MW01165468

OPUS ODYSSEY

A STORY OF SURVIVAL & PREPAREDNESS

BOYD CRAVEN III

Copyright © 2017 Boyd Craven III
Opus Odyssey, A Story of Survival & Preparedness
By Boyd Craven

Many thanks to friends and family for keeping me writing!
All rights reserved.

To be notified of new releases, please sign up for my mailing list at:
http://eepurl.com/cZ_okf

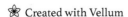 Created with Vellum

CONTENTS

PROLOGUE

"Sarge, it was like I told you. Other than hitting Dan, I didn't have to hurt anybody, the other guy just gave up. I sort of feel bad Casey died, but that was his choice, not mine. If I feel bad for other people's bad choices then I don't know if I could live with myself."

"So... despite a raging snowstorm, bad guys armed with guns and crowbars, and the dark, and cold, you kicked some ass, saved two grown assed men who never should'a been caught, and you led them home?"

"In a manner of speaking?" I said, somewhat confused.

"Congratulations, son. Of all the puckered assholes I've ever met, you walked into one side of hell and out the other. This time you were the last man standing."

"Sir? Your point?" I asked, not understanding any of that.

"You're not the only one. Now unlike you, I do feel bad about other people's choices sometimes. Especially yours."

"Mine?" I asked him, totally confused now.

"Yes, you see... this time, you were the last man standing, but what if something happened? What would that do to Tina?"

"What does she have to do with this?"

"If you had died out there, what happens to her? She loves you, don't she?" he asked, straight to the point.

"Yeah," I admitted.

"You love her." It was a statement, and not a question.

"Yes sir," I told him.

"Good. Don't be a puckered asshole like every other guy. Do the right thing and make her an honest wife. And if you let one word slip of this conversation, I'll be on you like flies on shit. You hear me boy?"

"I understand sir, and you're right," I told him, a grin tugging out the corner of my mouth.

"Now hand me that damned sandwich and wait here for five more minutes before telling the rest of them they can come back in."

NEXT WEEK:

Something zipped between us, like a bee on crystal meth with a raging case of diarrhea. The sound of the shot was only a heartbeat behind that.

We both dropped to the ground.

"Opus, get behind some cover," I screamed, as another shot hit a rock near my right shoulder, sending chunks my way.

"Go," Tina yelled, then shouted unintelligibly to the dog.

I felt something brush against me, and sand and rock chunks sprayed my prone form. Something was hot and running down the side of my head. I must be sweating worse than I thought, thinking that the bullets whizzing past us weren't at the firing speed that they'd been fired earlier. Opus had put his head down and was belly crawling to Tina.

These weren't hurried shots, and were barely missing, which was troubling and it made me feel funny in the pit of my stomach. The adrenaline was once again raging through my system and my ID was screaming fight or flight.

"Let's leapfrog the bushes for cover, he has to be firing at a distance—"

Another shot went whizzing past, hitting about three feet in front of Tina's head. She made her move, and I pushed myself to my feet and took off as two more shots came in. I never heard or saw where they hit, but I felt a tug at my pack as I slid to a stop near Tina, knowing something had happened, but my adrenaline and fear had me high as a kite, ready to run.

"Rick, you've been shot!" Tina said, crawling toward me.

RICK

I f you had told me two years ago that not only would I become a somewhat serious prepper, but that I would also meet a woman and fall in love with her, I might have called foul.

I didn't really enjoy a ton of other people's company and chose my friends carefully. Obviously, a lot has changed, and although I am what people consider an introvert, I just prefer quieter company to larger crowds. My love of camping and hiking went well with my ideas on prepping. Those, along with a string of events, had pulled Tina and me together.

It was my last week living at Al's. I would have left a couple of months ago, but his arrest had caused him to lose his job from missing too much work. I could have easily just given him a couple months' worth of rent and walked away then, but I wasn't sure he'd actually use it on rent if I gave it to him. Then again, it gave me time to adjust to the idea of how radically my life had changed. After the events of the past winter, I wanted something even more relaxed than my regular apartment lifestyle. There were too many people around me, and my greatest fears were still that there could be another bout of civil unrest.

"Hello?" I said, not recognizing the number on the caller ID.

"Hey, this is Sonja, is Al around by chance?"

I recognized her voice, but confirmation helped; I mostly remembered her as 'Taco Bell girl.'

"Naw, he said he was leaving for work an hour ago," I told her. "He's got a new schedule."

"Ah, if he's working, no wonder he isn't answering. Hey, listen, we were gonna go to a rally this weekend. Do you and Tina want to come with? We can snag some pizzas and beers later on."

"I'm not really into the kind of rallies you are," I told her. "But thank you. Too many people, anyways."

"You must really hate politics. I still can't believe you told Al to sleep with one hand over his butt till you got his dad to bail him out. He said he couldn't sleep for two days."

I had to laugh; it hadn't been one of my finest moments, and if I remembered correctly, I had also told him not to drop the soap. Gallows humor is what it was, not that I would ever wish that on anybody, but it was amusing to hear that it had bugged him. He hadn't mentioned it, so I had a little nugget of info I could use if I needed him to back off of pushing for a wedding date. *Sheesh*. I hadn't even talked to Tina officially about it since the hospital, where I'd gotten cotton-mouthed and written her a quick note. What we had talked about was moving in together, or me moving in with her.

"I do hate politics, but like I said, too many people. Besides, I'm moving, remember?"

"Oh, yeah. Well, after the rally, we could always come help you load up the big green creeper van and help you move!"

"Sure, call me when the rally is done. But, I don't know that I really have all that much to move. Almost everything I own is in one room and in—"

"The property up north," she finished for me.

"Yeah," I admitted sheepishly.

"No, I totally get it, I'm not picking on you. My dad was the same way."

"Was?" I asked her.

"He died... when I was twelve."

"I'm sorry," I told her. "I had no idea."

"Oh, don't be sorry, it was sudden, and it still hurts sometimes, but it is what it is, and it's not your fault."

The younger lady had a point, and although I didn't like politics, especially hers, she did show signs of wisdom and intelligence that I had missed when I had first met her. I'd thought she was just another string of one-or-two-date types of failed relationships that Al had been in for a while.

Yet, she'd stuck around. I'm not an easy guy to get to know, but she was trying to make an effort, something I just now realized.

"If the weekend doesn't work out, maybe we can have you both come out with Tina, Opus and me for some BBQ or something. The summer is almost here, and the mini-storage is kind of slow right now."

"Hey, I like that idea. How about we ink it in, with a TBD date and time on it?"

She sounded excited.

"Works for me. I'll let Al know you called, in case he forgets."

"Thanks, man! Later, tater."

Tater?

I hit end, and shook my head. I walked over to my small desk and woke up my Mac. Now that I had gotten a little bit known in the PNR categories (paranormal romance), I had started writing longer. My fans were asking for MOAR! Since I could write a 60,000-word book as fast as I could write two 30,000 word books, that was what I'd been doing lately.

I was using a program called *Vellum* to do the formatting and was happy when I saw a *Dropbox* notification that the file had been edited and updated by my virtual assistant.

I sent off a quick email to double check that everything was done, and was soon going through the corrections on *Word* while waiting for a response. My phone buzzed instead of getting an email back, and I saw the note my assistant had sent.

All ready.

Good, because one thing I'd noticed, the more I wrote, the cleaner the writing got. Every draft handed back to me had fewer corrections per word count, and it was improving. Which meant, as a writer, I was growing —I think. Sales had been slowly climbing, book after book, and I'd got some great press from a couple of bloggers.

One blogger had messaged me out of the blue on *Facebook* asking if she could review a book for me. I'd said sure, and then asked her if she wanted a review copy, but she said she'd already read it. I told her I would love a review; good, bad, or indifferent. Every review helped, and I looked at reviews as direct feedback from my core audience.

What I got was a video review. I was blown away, and her video review was shared far and wide. It was weird. I'd got a phone call from the local news station and was asked to do an interview. I'd politely declined, because cameras kinda freaked me out and I'd rather stay mostly anonymous.

Still though, having a book ready to go, making it my second full-length one this month, was going to do good for my bottom line. All this raced through my head as the editing side of my brain did the accept or reject changes. I finished it and then fired up the formatting software. That was the part I loved, yet it was only ten minutes of work or less to format a book using *Vellum* and have it ready for *Amazon* and a print version.

My VA would take the page count from the formatted print version, and we'd work on a blurb together, and she'd do the final coordination with the cover designer I'd recently found. After working with her off and on for a while, I'd given her the passwords to upload the books for me.

There is a lot of trust involved when you do something like that, but I'd had contracts drawn up by a lawyer. The VA would take care of the moving parts, so literally all I had to do was create the content, make suggestions on what I wanted on the cover, do final yay or nay on edits, format and then repeat. My content creation had finally gone through the roof by hiring out some of the work.

My phone rang again.

"Hey there," I said.

"You coming out tonight or what?" Tina asked.

"Or what," I told her.

"Really?"

"No, just finished work for the day. I was going to call you in about five minutes or so, but you beat me to it."

"Great minds and all."

"Yeah, I'll grab a shower and head over soon," I told her.

"Sounds good. Love you."

"Ditto, give my furry buddy an ear scratch for me."

"I will. Bye."

I hung up. I was going to grab a shower, but there were a couple more things I wanted to do before I went to her house, something I'd read about in a prepper group on Facebook. I fired up my Chrome browser and headed to Amazon. I ordered half a dozen LifeStraws, filters built right into a suction type straw, and a lock-pick gun. It was a Rube Goldberg-looking contraption, but people swore by them. I don't know why I'd ever need to unlock something I had a key for, but figured it was something I could use in a book, so it would be nice for research.

I updated the shipping address; I wouldn't be here when they came in.

RICK

Tina had my favorites out when I got there: her sourdough crust pizza and a six-pack of Budweiser. The day hadn't quite ended, and the mini-storage was still open, but there was a lot of slack time. Two customers were loading or unloading their units, but nobody had stopped in the office since the morning.

I felt something warm and wet on my leg and reached down to pet Opus, who melted under my hand into a puddle between the two office chairs Tina and I had slid next to each other.

"So, you're moving in."

"Yeah, you're excited, aren't you?" I asked her.

"Oh, I definitely am. But, you don't seem to be," she said.

Wait. Was this a trick? Some kind of Jedi mind-game, to lure me into sticking my foot into my mouth? Tina was one of a kind, but somehow I thought she might be testing me at this moment.

"I'm excited, but it's a lot of change. At least for me. I'm ready for it, though."

"It's pretty big for both of us," she said and put her hand in mine. I gave it a squeeze, and Opus whined from the floor.

I reached down to scratch his head. "Doc says you gained some weight while healing up your bullet wound. Too much loafing around, so I can't really give you any crust, boy."

Opus sneezed, the harshest condemnation he could give me. It suspiciously sounded like he'd said, 'bullshit'.

"You can have *my* crust," Tina said, and dropped him a generous piece.

He snatched it out of the air and wolfed it down.

"I was going to give it to him," I complained. "I just had to pull his chain some."

Opus leaned his head on my leg and licked his lips. I dropped a half-finished piece, and he caught it in mid-air. I wasn't the only one who loved Tina's sourdough, but it was filling, and I'd noticed that since I'd started to eat what I stored and storing what I ate, my eating habits had changed.

I was working out, and eating a more stable diet. That had helped me lean up and put on a bit of muscle; not that I was a bodybuilder by any means. But I did notice that I didn't wear out as fast anymore, and I could usually run laps around the mini storage with Opus and Tina without feeling like I wanted to die.

Then again, they usually did their laps twice a day, and I did mine once, but she was half my size, and Opus was a dog - a fabulously smart dog, who loved to run around to chase squirrels, and anything else small enough that he could catch and eat... or cadge some pizza from me.

"Don't give him so much, the cheese will make him stink!"

"Well, *I* don't have to smell dog farts for another few days," I said and then took my hand back from hers and poked her in the side.

She squeaked, and Opus stood up, looking at me sideways.

"It's okay buddy, just letting your mom know how much I love her."

"You still say it to the dog, but not me."

"See, Opus. She gets upset when I talk to you about the big deep issues. I think she's got a problem with confidence or something."

Opus chuffed.

"You both want to sleep in the doghouse?" she said sweetly, and then took the beers off the counter as a car pulled in in front of the rental office.

It was 5:50pm; close to closing. I looked at Tina. She shrugged. Another day, another dollar. The front doorbell jingled as it opened and a familiar-looking man stepped in. He looked around, and I saw him sniff the air, probably catching the scent of pizza. Behind the counter, we were visible, but Opus stood up, his tail giving a tentative wag as his mom greeted the visitor.

"Hi. Are you looking to rent a unit?" Tina asked, her usual opening.

"No, ma'am. You don't remember me, do you?"

"You look familiar," she said, hesitating a moment.

He was almost six-foot-tall, dark hair, sunglasses and wearing a suit. Now that I thought about it, he looked like he could be one of the agents from the Matrix. He took off his sunglasses and put them in an inside pocket, and then I remembered who he was.

"I was here about a year ago, when you had the armed robbery?"

"Detective Stephenson?" Tina asked.

"That's me," he said with a grin. "How's business?"

"It's steady. Not a lot of actual work right now, but people keep paying their bills."

"That's the kind of work I got to get into. Listen, I live just around the corner from here, and thought I'd stop out and share some news before heading home."

"I don't like the sound of this," I said quietly, and Opus whined, telling me he wasn't thrilled either.

"It's not good. The punk pled out," he said.

"We already knew that. Pled guilty, and was locked up."

"Yeah, but because of good behavior and time served, waiting for the courts, they let him out today. That's why I'm in this monkey suit and not in uniform. I testified against him. Prison crowding, yadda yadda yadda."

"Yeah, he was a two-time offender already, I thought it was three strikes?" I asked, noting no wedding band on his hand and the way he was looking between Tina and me.

"They plead his felony down. Anyway, like I said, I live right down the road, and I wanted to let you know, so you didn't get surprised by the news some other way."

"He's not... coming here, is he?" Tina asked.

"I doubt it," I said, and stood up. "Detective Stephenson is just giving us a heads up. I think he remembers your fuzzy buddy is on guard, too."

"I do," he said leaning over the counter and coming eye to eye with Opus, who let out a soft growl. The detective stepped back from the counter half a step.

"Don't worry, he's just letting you know that I'm claimed," Tina said sweetly.

"Claimed? You two? Congratulations! When's the wedding?"

Suddenly my shoes looked interesting... We'd vaguely and very obliquely talked about things, but I needed to man up and do what old Sarge said.

Before I could answer, Tina spoke, "Nothing is firm yet, but sometime in October. We both have birthdays then, and fall is our favorite time of the year."

That was news to me, but it sounded perfect. I didn't really have any family, and the friends I had could be counted on both hands. Tina, on the other hand, had family in Arizona that I'd yet to meet.

I felt weird. I wasn't scared of commitment, but something old fashioned in me had reared up after I'd written the note to Tina in the hospital. I felt that I needed to talk to her dad before I nailed down a date. I knew that sounds like a cop-out, but something *my* dad had told me before he'd died about how he'd proposed to my mom, was holding me back. I swallowed and fought back the painful memories.

Stephenson answered, "That's great!"

"If you want an invite, let us know," I told him. "I personally don't have many people to invite, but if Tina goes with a big wedding, I might need to beef up my side of the guest list a bit."

Tina looked at me in surprise, her mouth slightly

dropping down to her ankles, and Opus let out two chuffs back to back - an Opus laugh.

"I might just take you up on that. You having it around here?" Detective Stephenson asked.

I glanced at Tina and gave her a small smile. "We don't know. We have to talk, but the two places I have in mind are a little ways off. Either down in Arizona where her family is, or up north near Bud and Annette."

"Old Sarge," Tina said with a grin. "We need to go see them soon," she said, and touched my arm.

"I'd go right now, but I'm moving," I reminded her, and kissed her on the forehead, firmly planting my stake in front of the would-be suitor who grunted with indifference, letting me know message received.

He hurriedly planned his retreat. "So, I'll check back in a few days, once I know more. I don't think you have anything to worry about. He didn't seem to have any animosity toward you... three." He gave me a hard look, reiterating the fact that I was the one who'd thrown the superman punch, while Opus had made mincemeat of the robber's arm. He lightly tapped his fist on the counter. "I just wanted to let you know."

We said our goodbyes and that was it. Six o'clock had finally rolled around, and Tina hurriedly flipped the switch off on the open sign and locked the office door.

"So, you in a rush to get home?" she asked mischievously.

"No, ma'am," I replied, with a wink.

RICK

"Dude, I'm going to miss you, bro," Al said as he and Sonja helped me load the last of my flat storage totes into the back of the van.

"Same. I know you guys are going out again this weekend, but do you have any plans on Sunday night?" I asked.

"What?" Al answered.

"He's asking us to dinner you dummy, a barbeque," Sonja said with a grin.

"I like B.B.Q.," Al said, spelling it out.

I knew that he did. Sometimes, with a Hispanic and Italian family, his loafer-surfer persona clashed with his mid-Michigan roots. So many clashes, one little flesh stick.

"Well, I was going to try to cook some ribs on my new smoker on Sunday. Kind of a - it isn't a housewarming party when you move in with your fiancé, is it? Not sure what to call it."

"How about a relationship party, or something?" Taco Bell girl offered.

I shrugged. "Something like that. Anyways, if you guys want to come, we're firing up the smoker grill around noon. Food should be ready about six."

"We'll be there," Sonya answered for them both.

I slammed the back doors to make sure they wouldn't pop open, waved, and got in.

"You know, I always thought you had a limited wardrobe, but you *really* need to go shopping," Tina told me with a grin.

"I have my night-time pajamas, my daytime pajamas, and my going-out-in-public clothes. What more do I need? You can see what I wear mostly."

"Basketball shorts and T-shirts."

"Exactly," I said.

Opus chuffed his approval.

"Don't *you* go picking sides now," Tina chided him, and Opus laid down and put one paw over his nose. He was hamming it up.

The dog had slowed down after he'd healed, but that might have been more to do with age than actual pain. I didn't know why he'd warmed up to me even more since last year, but he had. He'd been showing affection more and more lately, treating me like an equal member of the family group he was in charge of. You don't own a dog, they own you.

I went back to unpacking my clothes. We'd put my futon into the spare bedroom at Tina's place, and moved my clothes into a new dresser she'd put in her bedroom just for me. Sure, I'd stayed over there, and she'd stayed at the apartment, and we'd both stayed in the motorhome at the bug out, but this felt different. The only thing I didn't see was somewhere to store my prepper supplies in the house, which is why I'd rented an actual unit for myself - despite Tina's objections.

Other than my clothing and futon, the only other really major thing to move was my computer stuff. I'd begun my career with a beat-up Asus that had taken me through college, until I'd dropped it, and then it was an HP that I still used, as well as a MacBook Air that had later been replaced with a Mac Mini and large monitor.

All of this fit into a tote, with the exception of the monitor, and I was putting off setting up my office. I stepped over to the spare bedroom and was stood in the doorway staring at the tote and monitor, when Opus pushed past my legs and jumped up and flopped down on the far end of the futon.

Tina slid up behind and wrapped her arms around me. "Penny for your thoughts?"

"That's no way to make money," I told her.

"What, sitting here with you?"

"No, begging a penny every time I think." I turned and returned her smile.

"So, what's bugging you?"

"Nothing. I just... I look at this room you set aside for me to work out of. I like it, but it doesn't feel *real* yet."

"No?" She asked, pushing me a little bit so we both could step out of the doorway.

"Well, I'm still here. Hey, this is day one."

"You want to set it up for you? Make you a man cave?" she asked.

"I don't have to have all that. It's just... God... for so long, I was alone. It was a couple of boxes of clothes, my futon, a desk, and a laptop. I could live out of my van, so I went camping a ton. Even though I was alone, I didn't feel lonely then."

"And now?" she asked, chewing on her lip.

"Now... I realize how alone I really was after all," I told her and pulled her close to me, "And, I'm just kind of amazed at all the changes. In a good way."

I bent to kiss her, but not before Opus jumped off the futon and bounded over, putting his paws on my side and sticking his fuzzy snout between us. The huge dog joined in, swinging his head back and forth, taking swipes at our necks and faces with his big wet tongue. I recoiled, almost falling, while Tina made laughing choking sounds.

She wiped her mouth and tried to spit the taste of dog slobber away.

I laughed. "Nice job buddy." I grew more serious. "But, do you want this to be like up north, where we close the bedroom door?"

Call me crazy, but the dog understood our words. He cocked his head to the side, and sneezed his disapproval.

"That's what I thought," I answered him.

Opus didn't trust Al.

Several times during dinner when Al got up to get a beer, or went inside to use the bathroom, he'd find his route back to Sonja blocked by Opus, who would give a low growl, standing in front of the woman.

This sent Tina into the giggles every time, and after a while, I realized Opus was just messing with him. The next time Al walked away, he shot Opus a baleful glare and instead came to stand near to me, where I was leaning by the back deck, watching the whole thing play out.

My fuzzy son stayed put.

"He doesn't like me," Al muttered.

"He does, actually," I told him, taking a pull from my beer. "That's why he's messing with you."

"Really? That's not cool, man. What does he think he's doing?" Al's easy-going persona disappeared, apparently really rattled by Opus's pretend aggression.

I shrugged. "I think he's trying to see if you're worthy of Taco Bell Girl."

"Dude, she's got a name," he told me, exasperated.

"I know. I do that to piss you off." I grinned. "She and I set this up when you were working late on Wednesday."

"I know you do, and it works. So, stop. Wait, you said he's trying to see if I'm... *worthy*? How smart do you think that dog is?"

I snorted. "If your college stories are true, he's probably at least three times as smart as you."

Al jerked his head up. "Hey!" he said, pretending to be hurt.

"Naw, he's smart. Seriously, dude. I'm just saying. I don't know if he understands *every* single word I say, but he understands most. How about you try talking to him and telling him why you deserve to be near Sonja."

Al squinted his eyes at Opus. He turned and snatched

my beer out of my hand and began drinking it, his eyes daring me to stop him. I grinned, and when he looked back to the dog, pulled another beer from the cooler I had stashed behind me.

Fresh beer in hand, I followed Al as he stomped back, stopping two feet away from Opus. He got down on one knee, and I cringed. I knew Opus was smart, but sometimes getting eye to eye with a predator could be construed as a challenge.

The dog tensed.

"Opus, my man," Al said, back in character, "I *got* to see my lady, and you're cramping my style, dude."

Opus continued to growl softly, but the tension had left his back legs.

"Listen, Bud. That there is my *girlfriend*. Someday, maybe it'll be more, like what Rick and your mom have. I don't want to screw things up, but I won't get a chance to find out if you keep me away from her."

Opus stopped growling and waved his tail a tiny bit. Then, he sat down on his back legs and looked up at Al.

Al smiled and turned to look at me, shooting me a thumbs up. When he turned back to the dog and Sonya, I gave *Opus* the thumbs up.

Tina and Sonja quieted, keeping their eyes on Al and Opus. Al swaggered as he strolled on by fur face, when suddenly Opus turned and let out a quick growl, and nipped at Al's butt.

Al screamed and fell over his lawn chair, the rest of the beer he'd stolen from me spilling. Tina and Sonja burst into giggles, and I walked over to Al. I held out a hand and pulled him back to his feet and fixed the chair.

"Sorry about that, brutha," I told him, "Told you he was messing with you."

Al wiped beer off his face. "Look at him. He's laughing at me, isn't he?"

"Yes," Tina said, and I turned to see Opus once again sitting in front of Sonya, tail wagging and mouth open, tongue out the side in the biggest doggy smile ever.

"He's laughing his tail off," I told Al. "Come on, your beer seems to have disappeared."

"It's practically alcohol abuse," Al complained. "You got a shirt I can borrow, bro?"

"Yeah, come on," I said, motioning to the house.

Before closing the sliding door off the deck, I looked back at Opus, happily sitting on-guard in front of Taco Bell Girl. The girls waved and grinned. I waved back and headed inside.

4

RICK

The radio played softly in the car, as Opus sat between us, headed north on US23/I75. We both were looking forward to a long weekend. It hadn't been a year yet since we'd officially got together, and I thought about her visit on the fourth of July last year.

Tina had drank only three beers at the campfire, and I'd had to carry her inside. She still remained a lightweight and hadn't tried a repeat performance. One was her limit, and even then, it was usually a half before she discreetly poured it out, or passed it to me.

I glanced down at Opus. "I bet you that General Zha and his squirrel minions will be ready to wage war with you, fur-face. Think you can actually catch one for once?"

Opus chuffed back at me in response, and Tina scratched behind his ears. He rewarded her with a pleading whine, so she did a more thorough job of it.

"What's the plan this summer?" she asked.

"Well, I figure after Dr. Brett fixed up old Sarge, we'd talk to him and see if he's ready for us to get hitched.

Maybe he and Annette have an opinion on where to go. Since I'm happy wherever you are, my vote doesn't count, but I'd like to see what they say."

"Your opinion does too count," Tina insisted. I could tell my frankness had surprised her.

"Well... I..." I hesitated. "My dad was a little bit old-school, from what I can remember. So, I kind of feel like I need to talk to Sarge, and then maybe get in touch with your father—"

"I *knew* you were holding back because of some macho bull like that!" Tina said, half amused, half annoyed, judging by her tone.

The tips of my ears burned. "I know. And we might not get as much time up north this year with all we have to accomplish in a short period of time, but—"

"—My Daddy is excited to meet you," Tina interrupted. "And Mom has seen pictures, and knows all about you too."

"Okay, how about after this long weekend, we get our go-bags ready and take a long vacation? Do a road trip and end up in Arizona?"

Tina chewed on her lip, and stared out the side window. "I don't know, it's about to be the busy season."

"Who do you have to watch the desk when you're sick?"

"My mom's girlfriend from college," she said. "She helped my mom run it when I was younger."

"Would she be willing to cover for you?"

"It's... eh... I don't know if the business can afford to hire somebody on for an extended period right now. Not unless we get a few more renters."

"I'll cover it," I offered. A low grumble of approval came from Opus.

Tina hesitated. "It's—"

"It's not that much," I interrupted. "And if you want to get married in the fall - like I do - why wait? You can only get married to me once, you know."

"Like, I'd marry you more than once," she joked, lightening the mood.

"No, most people don't repeat stupid acts," I joked back.

"You're... *grrrr...*" she answered, actually growling.

I grinned and turned down the road that led to Sarge's. In a few more minutes, we'd be there.

"So, who's this Zha guy? From one of your books?"

"Naw, kind of a take-off of on an old Superman villain named Zod or something. Opus seems to think that squirrels are the devil, so I gave his chief instigator a name last year. He hasn't been able to catch him yet, but I can just imagine a new brood of mutant ninja squirrels, ready to steal all the nuts, and pull on the dog's tail."

Opus let out an audible grumble from his chest, and I grinned, finally turning on the drive to Sarge's. I wondered if we should have called first, but decided not to as a surprise.

I was surprised all right.

We pulled to a stop on the drive that led back to my place, but in front of his house. Sarge and Annette were both standing at the railing of their back deck, waving. Sarge was standing there, his oxygen on, but he'd lost a ton of weight. He was big before, but he was pretty limited in his mobility and...

"Oh, wow," Tina said softly.

"You two want to go say hi first?" I asked as we waved back.

Opus chuffed, and Tina was already opening the van door. I followed close behind. Opus legged for a moment, finding a bush, then went ran, barking happily toward the older couple. He beat us there by several seconds, and Annette was laughing softly at the dog's antics. Opus stood on his hind legs, his front paws pulled to his chest, seemingly dancing in joy. Sarge was struggling to hold onto the deck with one hand, trying to pet the fuzzy moocher with the other while keeping his balance against the beast.

"Hi, you guys!" Tina called.

"Hi, yourself, get your skinny behind up here 'fore I sick my dog on ya."

"You don't have a dog," I called to him.

"He does now," Annette said.

Opus stopped dancing and stilled long enough to lay his head on the old man's shoulder.

"What a faker. He's going to get a Grammy for that performance," I whispered.

Opus dropped down on all to fours and sneezed in my general direction. I mentally sent him the thought, *I know where you sleep*, and he sat down, giving me a doggy grin.

"Look at you!" Tina said. "Are you okay?" She fussed at Sarge as I walked over and shook his hand. I gave Annette a firm hug.

"Better than I ever have been. Well, for a long, long time now," Sarge answered.

"He's still sore from surgery, but he's doing good," Annette said.

"What surgery?" I asked in surprise.

"Grab a chair if you two have a chance to sit. I might be in better shape," he said, "but I still get out of breath."

We walked to the small four-seat patio table and made ourselves comfortable.

"I didn't know you had surgery. When was this?" I asked him.

"Oh, about six and a half weeks ago. Went down to the Cleveland Clinic. Got a ton of my plumbing fixed. I mean the heart doc, not that the other plumbing has any problems..."

Annette snickered, and he shot her a glare that would fry an egg.

"I... I'm glad you're doing well," Tina said, "We just didn't know you had surgery."

"And you got *skinny*," I finished the thought she'd left unsaid.

"I wasn't fat to start with," Sarge insisted. "I was just a little rounded from being stuck so long and..."

Annette patted my hand. "Bud got a tingling in his hands again. I was worried he was going to have another heart attack, so we got him checked out. We didn't like what the doc had to say so we called his cardiologist, Dr. Brett, and he suggested the Cleveland Clinic."

"I thought you couldn't go under with your COPD?" I asked.

"Yeah, me too, but there are new techniques. If I had to have the VA pay for it all, I might have died waiting. As it is, it was worth every penny."

"Did they do the tummy tuck too?" I asked him, innocently.

"You little knob-gobbling, Johnson-yanking, pearl-clutching, no load—"

Annette interrupted. "No, but the strict diet they gave him has been followed since the sandwich incident."

"I got my eye on you, boy," Sarge said pointing.

I grinned back at him. "It's good to see you."

"Yeah, I missed your ugly face too. Even the demon dog. Only one on this property that knows what it's like going into a gunfight and walking out victorious."

Opus chuffed and laid his head against Sarge's leg, but he was watching Annette and then his mom.

"What about me?" Tina asked, noting that he forgot to mention her.

"Well, if I was about sixty years younger and hadn't already been hitched—"

"He missed you, but I sure as shit ain't gonna miss him," Annette said and poked two fingers into her glass of iced tea and flicked the droplets in Sarge's face.

"You would too," Sarge said, and the same old argument started up.

We listened and egged them on for a good ten minutes before finally waving our goodbyes and promises to see them at the diner in the morning. I'd get my jog in, have my writing done and be ready to roll long before the 9am breakfast time. As we rolled down our driveway, Tina turned to me.

"I want to grow old together like that," she said suddenly, and then turned slightly red.

"I do too, just less bickering," I agreed.

"That's not bickering, that's just... them clearing the air."

"With threats of dismemberment?" I asked, remembering the Lorena Bobbitt reference.

"Yeah, maybe we won't go that far." She grinned as we pulled in to see the motorhome just where I'd left it.

We'd come back up here as soon as we could, but it had been a while. I opened my door and was almost knocked over as Opus went charging and barking at the large oak tree down by the creek, chasing something fuzzy and red up into the tall branches.

"If he could climb trees, those little red ninjas would be in trouble," I said absentmindedly.

"He can climb, I just don't encourage it," Tina said.

I looked at her, and she shrugged, and then pointed at the front door of the RV. I dug out the key and unlocked it.

Upon entering, the small space smelled a bit like hot dust, so I set about opening some windows, while Tina opened the ceiling vents. When that was done, I did a basic rodent check and saw no evidence, so I went outside and turned on the propane and plugged in the electrical. Before we'd gone home, I'd had a truck come out to pump out the black and gray water tanks, and we'd winterized it. I'd never done it before, but we'd never really planned on camping in the middle of winter. I lit the pilot light on the water heater and checked to see if the condenser to the fridge was running from the outside hatches before heading back inside.

"Maybe we should clean out the filters on the air conditioners," Tina told me when I walked in. "I bet you that's where the musty smell is coming from."

"I can do that," I told her and then watched as Opus

streaked by the front of the motorhome, chasing fast after something.

"He's gonna catch something someday. Then what are you going to do?" I asked Tina, pulling her over to the couch and sitting down.

"Well, I'm not going to pull it out of his mouth when he's eating it," she said. "Good way to lose a hand."

"True," I agreed.

We sat like that for a while, the fan running from the AC unit, the door wide open, and watched Opus run and have fun. Other than the prank on Al, he hadn't been too puppy-like lately, but now, back here in nature, I could see his serious demeanor he usually wore like protective armor slipping away as he ran like a greyhound, on the heels of a gray blur. He went over into a tumble, and when he came up, he had a small rabbit. I almost shouted for him to stop, but it was over before I even registered it had started. He shook his head and in three gulps...

"Well, you hungry?" Tina asked me suddenly, hopping off my lap.

"Yes, ma'am."

We grilled steaks on a metal grate over the campfire and had a couple of beers each. Tipsy, we both headed inside, where Opus was put out that I locked him out of the back bedroom. The door wouldn't stay closed all night, but there was something in the air.

I put on *All Dogs Go To Heaven* on the TV in front, and held my finger up to my lips. "Shhh..." I told him, and shut the bedroom door.

I HAD EVERY INTENTION OF BEING PRODUCTIVE, BUT I SLEPT until I felt Tina stirring and then heard her alarm going off. Suddenly, we both tried to roll off the bed at once and got tangled, arms and legs locked together in the sleeping bag. I hit the floor hard with Tina falling on top of me.

Opus gave out a loud woof sound from the other room, and Tina was the first one free and she pushed the sliding door open. He rushed her, sniffing her, getting on his back feet and then rushed past her to check me out. I was getting untangled from the sleeping bag when his cold nose got me under my ear. I instinctively clenched my head toward my shoulders, and he gave the side of my face a lick, and then rushed out.

I got to my feet and walked to the door while Tina rushed to get decent. I wasn't worried, Annette wouldn't be back here, and I wouldn't be able to make the same mistake I did last year by the river from where I was at now. I opened the RV door, and Opus took off like a shot. He made it past the gravel pad before doing his business, but his head was up, and he was sniffing the air.

"You overslept," Tina said from behind me somewhere.

"Quite a bit," I admitted.

"Well, hopefully, you're not too exhausted. We have breakfast to go to."

"How much time do we have?" I asked her.

"An hour to get ready."

"So, we only need ten minutes for a shower and getting dressed..."

"Better not play with the dog too long."

I laughed softly and whistled for Opus who was chasing something down toward the water. I heard him change direction and left the door open and went inside. We hadn't unpacked last night, just spent some time together, so today I was actually cramping, I was so hungry. I was set on ignoring that for as long as I could when I came back in and saw that Tina was sitting on the couch, a look of concern on her face.

"What is it?" I asked.

"Message from Char."

Char was the lady who was running the mini storage for Tina while we were gone, as a trial run for a longer trip.

"She said somebody was prowling around last night and kept tripping the motion sensors. Didn't get inside the gate, but they set the light off by the office side and the parking lot side. Wants to know if she should call the detective and give him the security footage."

"Well, yeah," I said, but she was already thumbing a message back.

Words tumbled out of Tina's mouth worriedly. "Going to. I don't know Det. Stephenson's number, but she should be able to get to him. I don't even remember what that guy *looks* like. It could totally be random, or it could be—"

"Calm down," I said, and sat down next to her just as Opus came bounding inside, and then decided he was a lapdog and sprawled out across both of our laps.

Tina got up and paced the camper.

"Hey bud, your mom is starting to get scared. I need you to take her for a walk and calm her down," I told Opus.

He cocked his head at me, and I sighed. "Not that kind of walk; stick with her, she's a ball of nervous energy.

Till she hears back from her girlfriend, we won't be able to get any bacon."

"That isn't going to hold us up," she said and headed outside determinedly.

She knew how to use the outdoor facilities I'd built last year. It had worked better than we'd hoped, and that was one thing I'd double-checked before the moon came out: I had brushed off the seat for her and I'd also put a new roll of TP in there.

I hurried to the back to get clean clothing. "Cold shower for me, I guess," I muttered, knowing the solar shower hadn't had time to absorb the heat.

We were finished with breakfast at the diner when Char texted Tina back and said she'd got ahold of the detective. She'd emailed him the pictures, and he'd let her know that it wasn't the man who'd tried to rob us before.

Tina almost sagged in relief. It was still troubling, and the police would be coming out to take a complaint and get the paperwork started, but it was Stephenson who had really sealed the deal. Neither I nor Tina could recognize the guy either, but it was good in a way. Not that having some random dude walk the fence line of the business and our home was comforting, but it wasn't as terrifying as thinking you might have a set of crosshairs on your back.

"Well, now you don't have to worry," Sarge said, looking at my leftover biscuits and gravy, with an extra ration of bacon for the furball, who was now laying at his feet with a longing look in his eyes.

Of course, Opus tried to valiantly stay awake, but the one order of bacon he'd tried to wolf down, along with his mom's toast, on top of his morning kibble and another wild rabbit, nearly did him in. And he was going to be impossible to sleep in the same RV with, later on.

"I guess I'm not all that worried," Tina said. "I thought I was, but..." she looked at Sarge's half-finished fruit bowl and grinned. "It's not as scary as having to give up biscuits and gravy, with bacon on the side."

Sarge cussed, and Annette turned her head to the side as the waitress came up and passed me the bill. I noticed all three ladies were grinning from ear to ear, and I mouthed 'why' to Tina. She mouthed back, 'because I can,' knowing she was winding Sarge up on purpose.

"Thank you," I told our waitress, my card already palmed.

She gave me a wink. "Listen, Hun," she said to Tina, "Your pup there is famous around these parts. Folks would love to have him visit more."

"I... I was surprised you asked us to bring him in."

"Well, he's obviously a service dog. Well, a police dog, but you're not in the military or police no more. So..."

"I'm..." Tina stammered.

"Thank you," Sarge answered for her. "People around these parts need to keep our veterans close to their hearts," he said and dropped a wink at Tina, who had suddenly turned red.

"I didn't—"

"Your pup is a perfect gentleman, and the boss and I are honored to have him here. He eats for free."

"I can't argue with that," I told her, noticing she'd deducted one of the orders of bacon.

I knew I shouldn't have let her keep that false notion, but the waitress was sort of right. Tina wasn't a cop, and she'd never served, but her dog was a cop and a soldier in his own rights. He was also a hell of an example of what pure love and courage should be, and it humbled me to see others recognize what I thought I had only noticed. Actually, I kinda felt dumb.

"She's never served," I finally admitted as Tina squirmed. "But you're right. Opus here was bred and trained to be a service dog, could have been a police dog, but he's got the most important job in the world. Keeping my girl safe. Maybe someday we can get him a lady friend to carry on the genes."

I don't know whose eyebrows rose more at my words, Tina's or Opus's. He even did the ear thing where he used them like directional beacons to hone in on my words. Here I thought he was still asleep a few seconds ago.

Shows what I know.

"That's what I was trying to say," Tina said finally.

"I thought she was talking about me," Sarge said.

"You think everything's about you..."

I smiled and walked with the waitress to the register as I heard Tina chuckle. Sarge and Annette were going at it again.

"It means a lot to us. The last time we left fur-face alone up here, things didn't go so well," I told the waitress.

"I heard about that. Scary and tragic. I didn't know there was drug stuff happening up here, you know, other than the wacky tabaccy."

I grinned and shrugged. I avoided drugs and drug culture other than some old Cheech and Chong movies, so I was sort of surprised by what had happened last year as well.

"Yeah, but he's Tina's rock. He's been her protector for so long now that we try not to go anywhere without him," I told her, taking the pen and the receipt for me to sign. I pocketed my card again.

"Now it sounds like it's your job. Are you two going to move up here full time?"

"No ma'am, at least, we haven't planned it that way. I still have to ask her father for her hand, to make it official."

The waitress raised her eyebrows. "What are you waiting for?"

I hooked a thumb over my shoulder at the three humans and one canine who was causing a small ruckus, "Mostly them. Had to see how they were doing before we go on a road-trip. Arizona. Hopefully, it won't be too hot."

"Arizona in the summer? Wow. It's got to be near 120 degrees in the shade."

"Yeah. Hmm.... Guess I need to make sure my air is working then," I told her with a grin.

"Well, if you want some more coffee before ya head out, let me know."

I followed her gaze and saw Tina smiling and talking animatedly on the phone. She was one of those expressive talkers, and she was waving her free hand around as she spoke, like the person on the other end could see it.

I grinned at the sight, and Opus's attention was pointed up at Tina now, even though I saw Annette's hand under the table with a slice of pilfered bacon up as a bribe. He caught the scent, barely broke eye contact with Tina and gently took it, then resumed looking up.

"Thanks, I will," I told her and then walked back and sat down.

"...I know, Daddy. Uh huh. The 24th? Oh... That's fine."

I'd learned when Tina said 'that's fine', it means, *I'm very disappointed, and I will not pout, as that's beneath my dignity.*

She continued. "Oh no. I think there's this thing in Utah he wanted to go to, so we'll make a side trip out that way first then come down. Uh huh... Mom too? That's great! Yes, he's a good boy, his shoulder doesn't bug him much. Oh really? Yes, Daddy. Okay. Love you too. Bye."

I listened and wondered what thing in Utah she was talking about and then it hit me. I hadn't really pressed her on it, but I'd showed her the email and flyer I'd gotten from Preppercon. It was reportedly one of the largest prepping shows in North America, and it was in Utah. Salt Lake City, if I wasn't misunderstanding things.

"Oh, Daddy!" Sarge said in a falsetto voice, and Annette snickered.

"I'm still his little girl, so he'll be *Daddy* to me," Tina told him, and the pout she had repressed earlier came back out.

Sarge looked ashamed for a second and then Tina's pout changed, and she pointed at him, "Gotcha," she said, and cracked up again.

"What was that?" I asked her, curiously.

"Well, I know you were wanting to get on the road, but I guess my parents were invited on a cruise and want to push back the timing on us coming down. Mom's going to be gone for like five or six days, but Daddy is golfing with his buddies on some kind of trip."

"Push back our timing? We didn't have any firm plan—"

Somebody kicked me under the table, and I immediately grabbed my shin and saw the retreating foot. I was expecting Sarge's boot, but it was Annette's. I looked up at her, and she dropped me a wink.

Tina's brow scrunched up in concern. "I thought..."

"I'm kidding," I told her, figuring out that something had gone on and I had missed the memo somewhere. "I said after here, I just hadn't realized you were already moving the ball down the field."

"A football metaphor?" Sarge asked. "Boy, you're about as sharp as a rusty spoon."

"I'm just—" I looked around, confused.

"Gotcha," Tina said again and laughed at the expression on my face. "I just asked them when they'd be around because we were thinking about stopping out next week."

"Oh, I see."

"See, he learns fast," Annette said from across the table.

"I'm never going to win, am I?" I asked everyone.

Opus's mouth opened in a doggy smile, his tongue hanging out the side as everyone said at once, "No."

5

RICK

We spent the rest of the week planning. I did my routine, as normal, in the early mornings and then would take a jog down the long driveway to the road and back with Tina and Opus. It wasn't quite like the laps at the mini-storage, or an hour on the treadmill, but it was exercise for me, and I didn't have it in me to do as many laps as Tina did. She was like the energizer bunny on steroids, after working out on an elliptical for an hour or two.

Utah. I'd never been out west before. It seemed like a crazy fun trip, and a great way to put off talking to her parents, with the ultimate goal of gaining their approval. But Tina threw me for a loop announcing the trip to Utah for PrepperCon. Sure, we would be killing time, it would be one more week of paying for Char to watch over things but honestly, she was affordable. She was retired, had a pension and lived two houses down from the mini-storage; a fact I hadn't known before.

It would be almost a 2,000-mile side trip but the more

we talked about it, the more I loved the idea. It would be the three of us on the road, Michigan to Utah, Utah to Arizona and then hit the sights on the way back. Did I mention I was more excited for Utah because it delayed the fact I had to talk to her parents? The thought terrified me, but I wanted to do like the comedian said and 'git r done'.

"So, I know you've made and scratched out a dozen lists. What are we planning?" Tina asked me, flopping down in a camp chair near me by the fire pit.

"Mostly, what I want to bring with us on the trip beyond clothes and food. I got one of those Yeti plug-in coolers being shipped to the house, but—"

"You don't want to bring War Wagon?"

"I did at first," I said, loving the fact she knew the name of my motorhome and didn't hesitate to use it in a sentence. "But when you look at the gas mileage, it will use about three times as much fuel to get there, and it's an older model. I'm not sure I want to take her across the mountains without a lot of checkups, and we're leaving soon."

Tina grinned at that. "So, we'll take your creeper van or my truck?"

I gently flicked the tip of her nose, which made Opus sit up and stare at me. "I figured my van. If the weather sucks or we don't want to stop, we can always sleep in that. I'm just mentally preparing for everything. I want to bring the WeBoost, and I'm looking at emergency food as well as a two-week supply for when we're gone."

"What, are we going to go all Rambo during the road trip?" she asked, her eyebrow arching up with a smile.

"Naw, but you know my newer hobby," I said, referring to my last year of prepping. "I'd like to be ready for anything. It sorta came in handy last year."

"So, you go ahead and do that, and I'll get the motorhome packed up. Are we bringing it back to the mini-storage or leaving it up here?"

"Do you mind driving my van back?" I asked her, knowing she only slightly disliked driving my van, which was longer and harder to drive than her newer truck.

"No, I think I can manage it. Though, if I am going to drive it, I want you to have Opus ride with you so he doesn't try to crawl into my lap."

"We can do that," I said, adding a couple more items to my list.

Tina looked over my shoulder, and I could feel her hair tickling my neck. Opus chuffed from his spot across from me.

"You know, I made a three-day pack for my truck," she said, pointing to my list.

"You did?" I asked her, surprised.

"Yes, you know, I read up on things, and it just makes sense. Did you know about the older couple who went off the road two winters ago and were stuck in the ice and snow for three days?"

"I'm guessing since the way you worded that, they survived?" I asked.

"They did. They had an emergency candle, some bottles of water and some snacks. They lit the emergency candle during the night and kept it off during the day. With the way the car came to rest, they couldn't get out, and part of the car was buried under the snow, so they were stuck. Somebody eventually saw the car almost on its side and called the sheriff where they were surprised to find them both in pretty good shape, all things considered."

"That was a news article you shared on Facebook, wasn't it?"

"Yeah. It's what really got me thinking. So, if you want to plan for a couple of weeks, I don't mind. If you want to plan for more... two is one, and one is none."

I had to grin, and when she left to start the cleanup process, I was amazed that I had found somebody who fit in with my beliefs and lifestyle so easily. Opus thumped his tail a couple of times. He was sitting on the floor across from me.

"You want to go on a long road trip?" I asked him.

He stood up and barked.

THE MOTORHOME DROVE EASILY ON THE TRIP BACK TO THE mini-storage. Tina had gone on ahead of me a bit the last half hour of the trip and was already talking with Char when I pulled in. She unlocked the gate and waited as I parked it in a spot and turned off the big 454.

As soon as I opened the side door, Opus took off like a shot, barking happily. I hopped out, pulled the step out to make the small amount of unpacking easier, then went and plugged up into power.

The gate had been closed and I saw Char throw something. Opus leaped, catching whatever it was in the air, and landed. The fuzzy kid then sat on his back legs, but I could see his whole body wiggling in a restrained fashion as his tail wagged furiously. She held something out over his head, and although I was now walking toward them, I couldn't make out her words. They just came out as a murmur.

"What a little traitor," I muttered to myself as I realized she was giving the fuzzy mutt some sort of treat.

"Hey, Char's got some news," Tina told me.

I hurried the rest of the way over, causing Opus to look up at me sharply, his ears turning. I knew what he was thinking, I'd gone from an easy walk to a near jog, and he was looking around to make sure there were no problems that he hadn't identified.

As much grief and teasing as I liked to give the dog, I knew he had the same sardonic sense of humor as I did. And that was not me projecting feelings, you could actually see the moods. He had his own form of smiling, laughter, showing concern, disbelief, and agreements. He took the last treat from Char almost robotically, and sat up straight, waiting for me to get close.

"Hey, Char, what's going on?" I asked her.

"Well, we didn't have any more late-night visitors. Not any that were caught on camera anyway. That Detective Stephenson stopped by twice during this week, just to check on things. I guess he's taking the video clip to the station to see if anyone recognizes the prowler."

"They still don't know who it was?" Tina asked, a slight frown on her face.

"No, and I sent you the pictures. Was it anyone you recognize?"

Tina looked at me, and I shook my head no.

"No, nobody I know. It's really hard to make out their features though. Could be anybody."

"How do you know it's not that guy that tried to rob you last year?" Char asked.

"The guy last year was about twice as big. Broader in the shoulders and chest, and lots of tattoos. What little skin we can see on this prowler here," I said, pulling my phone out and flipping to the picture that had been texted to me, "doesn't really look like there's any ink on this guy."

"If it's even a *guy*," Tina said, walking up next to me and bumping me with her hip.

"What do you mean, Hun?" Char asked.

I looked at her, kind of surprised. Char was probably close to the same age my parents would have been. She was in her late fifties, early sixties. Young for retirement, but loving life. She was half a head taller than Tina, so she was nearly eye level with me. She brushed a lock of hair behind her ears, as for once the breeze was blowing.

"Well, the figure was slim. I know we saw a face, but for all that I know, it could also be a *lady*."

I hadn't thought of that, and Char hadn't either. "Looks too tall," Tina said after a moment.

"That's what the good Detective was saying," Char said with a wry grin.

"Oh?" I asked her.

"Last time he came out, when I offered to take him to dinner."

"Char!" Tina said abruptly. "What... I mean..."

"He's not that much younger than me," Char said, blushing.

"He's—"

"He said *yes*," Char interrupted.

I couldn't help it, I burst out laughing in both humor and relief. I had thought he'd been sniffing about when he first came in. Something about him looking at Tina had made me feel all... *stabby*. Maybe I should do a quick re-write and not kill off the character I'd written him in as, or at least change the name and occupation. But Char looked like the cat that ate the canary, and I would never begrudge somebody falling in love... or whatever else it was.

I grinned as both women began talking in a rapid-fire style I recognized, and figured that it might take a couple minutes. Or an hour.

"Hey Opus, you want to go inside with me?"

He chuffed and walked toward the back door. Like a well-trained human, one owned by a furry buddy, I followed. Once we were inside, I peeked to make sure the office was empty, but Opus was already rounding the desk, heading back toward the living area. I walked back to the door past the office restroom; the door that separated the house from the business. Opus let out a whine and looked at me as I reached for it.

He growled.

Startled, I stopped and took an involuntary step backward, trying to figure out what he was telling me. He sniffed the crack under the door, still making a low growling murmur, though not the one I usually heard when he felt there was a physical threat. This was a vocalization I hadn't heard before, more of... *an anxiety sound?*

I wasn't sure. I saw the fur along his spine had raised some but was already starting to lay flat again.

"You smell something, buddy?" I asked, seeing him looking at the handle like it was hot, then going back to sniffing around the bottom.

Opus glanced at me and went back to work with his sniffer.

Outside, I could hear Tina laugh. For a second, the stab of anxiety I suddenly felt was gone as I realized how much in love I was with this woman, but then Opus whined, bringing me back to the present.

"So, maybe Char had to run inside. Is that who you smell on the door?"

I received a stare in response, so I reached for the handle and twisted it. The door opened and...

Nobody jumped out at me.

The door separating the business and the living area opened into Tina's kitchen. The wall of pantries along the left wall was almost absolute and held her favorite ingredients and dry goods. Along the right side was her fridge, followed by a long stretch of countertop, the stove, then it turned a ninety-degree angle for the sink and a small snack bar.

I saw an empty water glass on the edge of the sink, upside down. I knew we'd loaded the dishwasher and run it before we'd headed up north and I realized that Char must have come in here and needed a drink.

I sighed in relief, but I was still curious. I mean, in my old life of like... a very short period ago, my room was my sanctum. Shared space was shared space, but now everything was shared space.

Opus ran around sniffing everywhere, but that was pretty much par for the course. I watched as he ran from corner to corner and then bounded off toward the living room that was immediately behind the kitchen. He did a small circle and then jumped up on the couch. He looked out the window for a moment and then hopped down and went running to Tina's bedroom. I followed him, not in a rush any more.

As my anxiety and, I will admit, a moment of fear abated, I was able to let out a deep breath and let Opus do his job. He found me just as I was nearing the bedroom door, and bounded into the office.

My office.

That sounded weird, I'd have to get used to calling everything ours, hers and ours. I opened the door to the bedroom and looked around. Nothing seemed out of place or sorts, so I let out a breath I hadn't realized I'd been holding. Opus ran in and jumped up on the bed and flopped. When I flop on a bed, I usually just drop straight down. When Opus flops, it looks like the dog did a leap and came down on his side, right in the middle of the pillows.

"You get hair all over your mom's sheets, she's gonna skin you alive," I told him, and he chuffed back at me.

I headed into the office next and checked everything out. Nothing looked out of place either, but I saw that my Mac was on and the screen saver was off. Had Opus bumped the desk and triggered the mouse or keyboard? I didn't have it locked, so I sat down and looked at what was on the screen.

My chrome browser was open to YouTube.

My arms broke out into gooseflesh. *Every breath you take*, by *The Police*, was paused.

I exited the browser, seeing that my remote login utility TeamViewer had been recently closed, too.

Opus came in and laid his head in my lap as I furiously typed. I double-checked all my data was there and that it was backed up on my Dropbox cloud before I did a virus scan. After that, I started the process of changing all my passwords on everything.

Since everything I do is digital, including my banking and shopping, I fixed that first. I was still going when I felt Tina wrap her arms around my shoulders, kissing me on the side of the head.

"You get lost in here?" she asked.

"Somebody logged onto my computer," I told her without looking up, making sure I had the last of the passwords changed from my checklist of logons.

"You mean, somebody other than you?"

"Yes."

"That's creepy," Tina said. "Hackers?"

"I don't know. I don't know if there's any way to access things unless..."

"What?" She asked.

"Somebody was inside here?" I asked her, "Still, I changed all the passwords."

"You think somebody was in *here*?"

"I'm pretty sure Char was at least in the kitchen. I'm not saying—"

"—Char wouldn't get onto your computer, I've known her since I was a kid!" Her voice sounded a bit angry and a lot hurt.

"I'm not saying it was her. What if it was..."

"Oh God, you're going to freak me right the flip out. *Don't*," she warned and stomped out of the room, barely audible.

Opus left with her, and I realized that there was a lot I needed to catch her up on. Opus's behavior, the glass near the sink, the creepy video left up on the screen of my computer, and evidence somebody had logged in.

She seemed upset I would even think it was Char, which I didn't... but I wanted her to cool off. Opus could tell she was upset, so he was going to stick close to her. He knew right now she needed him as she fought with the thoughts of somebody breaking in here.

I should have thought of that.

Her ex had terrified her, and before he was jailed, he had stalked her. Tina had never felt completely safe after that, and Opus had been purchased as a trained young dog who had finished his training and classes with Tina. I had really stepped into it now, potentially opening the floodgates to Tina's fears again.

I turned back to my computer, closing it out and decided to re-pack the van. We were going to head out early, and maybe I could talk to Tina in a little bit, smooth things over. I just didn't want to worry her that maybe the guy who was trying to break in, had come in here. I would have to think about how to broach that subject, but luckily, packing tonight for the trip out west would give me ample time, though half of my checklist was already in the van, most of the rest in the motorhome. I could get 90% of the packing done quickly.

I felt under the desk and put my fingers on the keypad and unlocked the gun case. By feel, I could tell my Beretta and two extra magazines were right where I'd left them. I didn't always carry it, though I was going to make that a habit now that I had my CPL.

Opus barked in the other room.

I locked the case to head over and see what they were up to and started to pack.

6

TINA

Tina really wasn't mad, but it had unnerved her to have Rick surprised and showing a little bit of fear. She worried that her reaction might have given him the wrong idea, but she knew, like any small disagreement, if she waited, he would come to her when he was ready. She knew she should reach out to him first, but she'd never really talked about the strong, brave face she wore.

To her, it felt like a mask. She worried that she overcompensated to beat her fear into manageable chunks. She'd told him about her ex, Lance, and he hadn't run screaming away. That was one of the darkest secrets. Yet, during the trial, she had avoided the media exposure. She was brought in as a witness, but the media had painted her as just another victim. What Lance had done still haunted her dreams, and she would have been the next in a long string of victims - if she hadn't escaped and had him arrested.

Still, she didn't want to confront Rick yet to apologize that she felt ashamed sometimes. Ashamed that she still felt vulnerable. He was her rock and had helped give her back the confidence that she'd lost.

She'd copied his list and when he'd gone outside to move items from the motorhome to his big van, and she started on the things inside that she could do to help.

"Opus, you want to help me pack some food?" Tina asked.

The big goof chuffed at her and she grinned, loving that the only other male creature that wasn't her father or her fiancé made her feel so safe.

"Okay, do you want to start with the bacon?" she asked.

Opus's tongue lolled out the side of his mouth and he seemingly shook his head.

"Don't tell Rick," she said, pulling out a package of bacon they would have to toss soon anyway.

Opus whined in anticipation as she peeled three slices off and put them between two paper towels, then on a plate. The microwave dinged a minute later and she put the plate on the counter to cool, dodging the furry missile that wound between her legs, tripping her up.

She pulled down the foods that they'd planned for the trip. She knew the staples and she was relieved that Rick had been eating healthier lately. She wanted him around a long time, and he hadn't really complained about jogging with her any more. He still loved going to the gym, but she thought that had more to do with the TVs and the noise that would drown out his obsessive need to squeeze every moment he wasn't spending with her, creating worlds.

Opus whined again, and she followed his gaze to the counter.

"Oh, all right," she said, and pulled the top paper towel off the bacon and held a strip up. "It's still a little hot."

Opus gave out a quiet bark and Tina rolled her eyes at his impatience before dropping it. He caught it in midair and devoured it.

"Not too fast, I don't want you burning your tongue," she said, before turning and pulling down spices to pack.

Opus gave a small moan, so, with a sigh, she grabbed another piece of bacon and held it over his head. He sat down, his back legs tensing, his front legs barely on the ground.

"Who's a good boy?" she asked.

Opus whined in impatience, and was ready for when she dropped it. She did the same thing with the last piece before putting the plate on the ground, wadding the paper towel up before throwing it in the trash can. She'd have to remember to leave a note for Char, asking her to take the kitchen garbage out in a couple of days so it wouldn't smell when they returned. Opus did his part to help, licking the plate eagerly.

HER ARMS WERE FULL, AND SHE WAS LOSING THE LAST OF her energy for the day. That in itself was surprising, but they had been on the move for the last hour. Rick hadn't talked about the incident where he'd sort of implied Char might have been messing with him. Instead, he'd talked about the upcoming trip. Her mind was in free-wheeling mode, trying to pay attention.

Her father would probably like Rick. He was quiet,

but when a gun had been pulled on her, she hadn't had to wait to get out of the situation herself, though she could have. She'd seen her fiancé jump over the desk like a TV detective and nearly knock out the guy who'd been holding her up.

What was his name again?

She couldn't remember, and had been worried that, with Lance's notoriety, somebody might have put two and two together when she'd been robbed at gunpoint. It had barely made the news, but nobody was paying attention to her, which suited her fine. She didn't want that spotlight.

Rick also hated the spotlight, but his career had skyrocketed and she was proud of him. She was at a loss sometimes on how to show him, or tell him. She definitely had fun watching him squirm when she was messing with him about it. That was when she had the idea. It might not only help her get him to come out of shell a bit, but it would also get him more exposure that might help him with book sales.

She would live blog the trip, something she knew his readers would love. Once in a while, she would be contacted by a fan of his, asking if she minded if they sent her a friend request. She trusted him completely, so it was kind of funny and she almost always said yes, with the exception with new profiles... no friends... and had profile pictures that looked to be glamour shots from the 1980s. She'd found out that these were almost always a scammer and did her best to protect him.

Which brought her back to her thoughts of her father. Rick was confident, but something about meeting her parents seemed to have unnerved him. Was it because he'd lost his parents so early? She knew her father would approve of him, even though he'd hated everyone else.

"I'm getting tired. I think all we need now is your go-bag," Rick told her.

"I'll grab it," she said, and turned to walk to her truck.

"Do you want anything else to go with it?"

Tina considered his question.

She shook her head. "I can't think of anything. We've spent a week planning it."

"Is there anything you'd like to see on our way there?"

"I'll see when we are on the road. I really don't know."

"Fair enough," he said, and watched her walk away.

Both of them hoped they could put the faux-argument behind them, but neither had mentioned it.

7

RICK

We got everything all squared away at the house, and I finished the packing without sticking my foot in my mouth too horribly. Tina and Opus gladly climbed into the van to go on a road trip, one I'd been sort of looking forward to, but was still scared of.

I checked everything off the list I thought we might need; sleeping bags small foldable air mattress that would easily fit in my backpack, kitchen utensils, different ways of cooking food, two five-gallon jugs of water.

Tina didn't even raise an eyebrow when I showed her. I loaded up the van with two of the one-month buckets of freeze-dried food that I'd ordered from Amazon. They supposedly contained a month's worth of food for four people, but I never believed that. I had set out to try those before, but never really had the occasion to do it.

"Does your dad know that you want to ride up front?" Tina asked Fur Face.

Opus let out a chuff, and came up and put his nose

under my right arm. I lifted my arm up like my fuzzy buddy wanted and scratched his ears, and looked over at Tina who shot me this 10,000 watt smile. I had to grin back, it was too difficult not to.

That woman had my heart, all of it.

"You're my buddy, aren't you?" I asked Opus.

He chuffed in answer, and I give him another scratch before putting both hands on the wheel.

"So, Tina, about what happened yesterday..." My voice trail off waiting to see if it would darken her mood or not.

"I know, I know. You explained. Do you really think it was the guy that was trying to break in the mini storage?"

"I never really said it was. It's just that Opus was hesitant about going inside the house when we returned. He made a growling noise and he was trying to tell me to stop, or proceed with caution. He hadn't done that before. And then I get that creepy message on the computer... It just threw me off. If it was just Char coming in to get a glass of water, I wouldn't care."

"I wouldn't care either," Tina told me, she was still smiling so I knew I was okay.

"I know she wouldn't have done that to my computer. Maybe it was just a bored teenager somewhere out on the net who guessed my password, and the rest is a weird set of coincidences."

"I thought you didn't believe in coincidences?" Tina asked. When I looked over she was grinning at me again, poking fun at me in her own way.

"Usually," I told her, "but if Opus hadn't been on edge, I would have chalked it up to that. I dunno."

We'd had an early start to the day, which for me meant about four hours ago. An early start to the day for

Tina was just about before 9am. Since the mini storage didn't open until 10am, she was never late. We both ran on our own different versions of the internal clock, just mine was wired for me to sleep really crappy, and to wake up at the crack of dawn. Since it was my favorite time to write and my most efficient time to write, it worked out.

Leaving between eight and nine o'clock in the morning from the Flint area meant that we ended up missing rush-hour traffic trying to head south on US 23. For a moment, just a fleeting one, mind you, I'd thought we were going to be stuck in slow traffic.

Instead, I had a notebook out, where I'd hastily scrawled the other two outlines the night before. Tina and Opus curled up, with Opus laying on the passenger seat while Tina leaned against the window. It wasn't long before both of them were snoring softly, succumbing to the mesmerizing effects of being on the road. I took the opportunity to get some writing done, via my recorder. I would look at my outline, read a sentence I wrote about my scene, and I would dictate it. Writing paranormal romance, eventually, I got around to where there was going to be a sex scene. I dictated that, from the female point of view.

Suddenly, Opus made a chuffing sound and pushed himself away from Tina. I looked over to see her entire body shaking. Her body was shuddering in mirth.

"Hey, what's so funny? You okay?"

"Yes, I can't believe... Just hearing your mouth say..." Her voice came out in a squeaky falsetto version of herself, imitating me, "and then he ran his hands up my silky thighs..." She laughed out loud, and Opus made another grunting sound, and sat up and looked at her.

I tried not to turn red-faced, but it was a little difficult. As long as we'd been together, even dancing around the issue of marriage, moving in together and everything else, I didn't actually think she'd read any of my stories. I guess she must have read *some* of them, but she'd never mentioned it, not really. That in itself, hearing her laugh, I suddenly realized how ridiculous it must sound coming out of a quiet, shy guy like me.

There I was, turning into a runner and a workout junkie like Opus and Tina, while having a voice that sounded a little bit like James Earl Jones narrating sexy times between a man and a woman... from a woman's point of view.

On top of that, I was a bit of an introvert. I just didn't like to be around a bunch of people, and I never liked to be in the middle of the drama. Everything that had happened in the last year wasn't typical of my life, I never got involved in things like that. So, to hear me dictating sexy times, she must've been dying over there. I could only guess how long she'd been listening, and how long I'd be teased about it.

"Yeah, yeah, laugh it up. I do what I gotta do to pay the bills," I told her with a grin.

"So, you're a pimp with your views." Tina snickered.

"Yeah in a way I guess. I mean the stories are kind of fun to write, but after a while, you get bored writing all the sex scenes," I told her seriously.

"Why don't you write about something else?" Tina asked. "If you're getting bored or tired of writing them, write something different."

I opened my mouth to disagree, then realized she was right. What if I could write about something else? I was about to ask her what she thought would be fun when I saw flashing lights in my rearview mirror.

There was a Michigan state patrolman coming up fast and hard behind me. I let off on the gas pedal noting that I was not speeding. I watched the mirror for a second, and Tina noticed my preoccupation, so she looked in her rearview mirror as well.

"I don't think he's—"

"No, he's got the guy in front of me," I said, watching as the trooper passed to the left of us. I slowed down so he could pull into the right lane in front of me, right behind the semi-truck in front of us.

Opus barked and wagged his tail, and licked me on the elbow before turning and licking Tina on the arm.

"You're a good Opus, you know you are," Tina cooed.

AFTER STOPPING FOR GAS, WE GOT BACK ON THE ROAD again. We were crossing Illinois when I got the idea. Writers are supposed to be normal everyday people. The truth of the matter was, they were all just a little bit introverted, but we have the superpower we can do really, really well.

This power is being able to *write*.

Writing a story isn't just enough to be a good author. I'm not talking about prose or grammar chops. What I'm talking about, is the ability to finish a story. I looked at everything I had been doing... Romance, romance action, thriller's, mysteries... Romance was really the only thing that had paid off so far. What I was starting to wonder was, if I could make my ideas and old genres mesh together even more. I spent some time thinking about that.

Tina said, "Did we just cross the Mississippi River?"

Pulled out of my thoughts, I looked up and saw the sign. I'd barely been paying attention to the changes in the road, I'd just been following the muted directions of the GPS. We'd gone from US 23 to 94 and had now been on I-80 West for some time.

"Sure looks like it to me," I said, looking around.

"I guess I knew it came up this far, but the only other time I've ever crossed the Mississippi River was near St. Louis, Missouri," Tina said.

"What did you do, go down there when your parents first moved?"

"Sure, just one instance. But I've traveled all over."

I'd spent almost my entire adult life living in Michigan, traveling around to short trips here and there, but this was my first time making a multi-week road trip like this. It would take us four days to get to Salt Lake City, Utah. I could make it easily in two days. Depending on what Tina and Opus wanted, we could definitely put in as many miles during the day and see the sights as we went.

"You know something I forgot to ask you. Is there anything along the way you'd like to see, in particular?" I asked Tina.

"Well, now that you mention it..." She hesitated, letting her words fall off.

"Yeah? What is it, we got all the time in the world to go see stuff."

"Well, this is going to sound silly, but... I want to go see the world's biggest ball of twine."

I looked over at her to see if she was serious, and laughed at her expression. She was sticking her tongue out at me and making faces.

"I don't even know what there is along the way," I admitted to her. "If you want to goof around, we've got plenty of time and places to do it."

"Well, we have all this camping gear. You want to just take it slow, camping along the way?"

"We can if you want. I'm also good with just a hotel wherever we end up."

"You know what Sarge would have to say about that, don't you?" Tina asked me sweetly.

"Probably tell me I'm wasting some kind of opportunity, for something, or something."

"No, that's probably what Annette would tell you. Sarge would probably tell you to take me back into the bushes."

I busted up laughing. Her voice had grown worse and raspy. Hearing the caricature voice coming out of a tiny woman like Tina made me grin.

Opus let out a happy bark as put his paws up on the dash. I ran my hand up and down his coat a couple of time giving him a good scratch and then looked back at my phone that showed I had email.

I pulled my cell phone from the cavity on the left, next to the driver's door, and looked over at Tina. "You mind taking pictures with my phone? If you post it on my Facebook account as we go, the fans I've got might be interested in following along." The last I said softly, feeling like a social reject for even bringing it up.

Tina's eyes got wide, and she immediately snatched my phone out of the center console where I'd placed it a moment before. "I wish we would've gotten a picture crossing the Mississippi River," she said immediately snapping pictures. "But I won't... you... I mean *I* won't tag the locations in my posts. That way if there are any creepers—"

"What? Creepers?" I interrupted, grinning.

"You know... as always. Creepy people. *Creepers*. The Annie Wilkes type of people."

"Misery? I didn't know you're a Stephen King fan."

"I'm a reader. But now that we're living together, I don't get my Kindle out as often and read."

I raised an eyebrow comically, and she just smiled back at me, me trying to look like the rock.

"You know, I did read one or two of your books," she told me with a grin.

I wanted to look over, but traffic was starting to get heavy.

"Which ones have you read?" I asked her without looking up.

"*Bearing the Mistresses baby*," Tina said with a grin. "I'm not sure how someone does that exactly?"

"You see, back in Victorian times..." I looked over for half a second. She was smirking at me, trying not to laugh.

Man, it was going to take me some time getting used to talking about my work and my writing, even with the woman I loved.

I reached over and grabbed her hand over the top of Opus's back. He chuffed at me sniffed at my arm and then lay down in the space between the two seats.

"You know what, Tina?"

"Yeah?"

"I just wanted to tell you... like I always told Opus... I mean, telling Opus is one thing, but I haven't really told you even though you know how these things go, and I haven't really figured out what I want to... What I mean is... I just wanted you to know how much I really, really—"

With a loud bang, the rear end of the van swerved across the highway.

8

RICK

W e were sitting on the far-right shoulder of the highway. Opus sat near Tina after doing his business while I wrestled with the big tire. The nice thing about having a one-ton Dodge Ram, is that you can carry, tow and load anything. The bad thing about having a one-ton Dodge Ram is that my tire had seven lug nuts and not five. The other problem with a big van was that it wasn't the regular 32 pounds of pressure. By the time I had got a flat tire off and on, I was just about done, and for the day. Tina had been sitting in the van with the motor running the air conditioning for a while, before turning off the van and coming out, sitting next to Opus in the shade.

"Hey, did you know that posting pictures and commentary while you're driving is giving you a lot of Facebook attention?" Tina asked me.

"No, I had no idea." I hadn't been checking my phone at all.

She had been taking pictures and typing updates; I'd

seen some, but only a couple. She had taken a video of me trying to change the tire on the big van and had caught me in a pretty funny exchange just a moment before. I'd smacked my knuckles and cursed some. Opus had just laid down and put his paws over his nose when he'd heard me. Tina had said that people would definitely hear her laughing as she had made the video live on Facebook. Let her have her fun, for now - I was going to take that one down later on in the day when she wasn't looking.

I finished checking all the lugs and opened up the side door before tossing the jack and the four-way inside.

"Opus, my boy, get up."

He jumped in and, before I could close the door, Tina hopped in behind him. I gave her a playful swat on the hind end, and closed the door behind her, smiling as she yelled and shook her hand at me.

I looked at my knuckles as I went around to my side, watching for coming traffic. I hadn't broken the skin, it was tender, not bruised. It was something I'd been careful about avoiding, as much as possible, resting my hands, especially the last couple years as my writing career had really taken off. I could hardly afford to break them or spend weeks without typing, though I'd done a lot more dictating lately.

I got in the car, rather I should say I opened the door to get into the van to see a big fuzzy mug pounce and lick me in the face.

"*Ugggg*," I said. "Get off me," I said, pushing Opus back. He gave me a happy bark and wagged his tail.

"Opus," Tina said, obviously the mastermind of this sneak attack. "You know he hates dog spit in his mouth."

Opus chuffed and wagged his tail some more, but he got out of the driver's seat. I pushed him back a little bit more, and he reluctantly jumped down into the space between the two seats.

"You ready to go?" I asked, firing the van back up.

"Of course!" Tina said.

THERE WASN'T ANYTHING BETWEEN MICHIGAN AND Nebraska that had Tina tied in knots to go see. Instead, she took pictures with my phone, sometimes video, narrating our trip but careful to keep herself out of the frame. I was itching to get some more dictation in, but I didn't want to interrupt her fun.

Opus had slept a lot of the ride in obvious boredom, so when I saw a sign for a KOA campground outside of Lincoln, I put my blinker on.

"Stopping for more fuel?" Tina asked, leaning over so she could look at the gauges.

I was about to answer when Opus lifted his head up, and his long tongue got her right on the side of the face.

"*Gah!*" She jerked her head back toward her side, wiping the slobber off.

"Good boy," I told him, knowing he would understand the concept of payback, even if it was hours later.

"What's he a good boy for?" Tina asked, with the eyebrow thing going again.

Opus let out a low whine, one that conveyed his anxiety.

"Nothing," I lied for both of us and he put his head back down, his lips pulled back into a doggy smile.

"So....?"

"Fourteen hours on the road. After changing that tire, my back is wrecked," I admitted.

"*Ahhh*, so I guess you won't want to stay up too late tonight?" she said coyly.

"I'm not sure I even want to put a tent up tonight," I admitted.

"Well, you said the back two bench seats fold down into a bed. Would it be hard to..."?

I laughed a moment because I only had one row left in the van, the other two had been out for years now. I did have a plan though, one hopefully she would like, and it wouldn't mean changing anything around much.

"No, we just need to pile the soft stuff on the buckets and totes that are on the passenger side."

"Air mattress?" she asked, hopefully.

"More comfortable than even the motorhome."

Her hand snaked its way into mine as I turned and followed the signs to the campground. It didn't take us long, and it was already dark out. I pulled up in front of the sign that pointed to the manager's spot. It was a fifth wheel, with a nice gleaming Ford truck parked next to it. The fifth wheel had fiberglass steps leading up to the door, showing that at least during a good chunk of the year, the management lived in the trailer here, probably not through the winter though.

I got out, hearing Opus scrabble into my seat where he could see better.

I'd grabbed my cell phone and walked up to the sign where there were leaflets in waterproof clear poly boxes. I turned on the flashlight app and read the sign, seeing I was past hours for checking in. I was reaching to pull out a leaflet when I heard the door of the fifth wheel open and the sound of Opus giving me a quiet warning bark.

"You're a little late for check-in," an elderly man's voice said in the darkness.

I turned and turned off the flashlight app and walked toward the voice, praying I didn't trip over anything since my night vision was already ruined.

"We've been on the road all day. I had a flat tire, or I could have been here a couple of hours ago. Is there a motel or hotel nearby?" I asked, already resigned to the fact that my day wasn't as close to being finished as I had thought.

"Naw, and you didn't pull no trailer. You wanting to pitch a tent in the dark?"

"To be honest, I was just going to throw up an air mattress and sleep till the morning and get back on the road," I said, feeling a tiny spark of hope.

"How many of ya are there?" he asked, stepping forward close enough so I could see him.

The old man was standing on the bottom step, and now that he was out of the shadows I could tell he was a little bit older than Sarge and Annette, though where Sarge was a bear of a man, this gentleman was on the tall and thin side. I could see his teeth flash in the dark as he asked me the last bit.

"Me, my fiancé and our dog."

"What kind of dog?" he snapped back immediately.

"German shepherd," I said quietly, "He's very well-trained, and he won't be a bother."

"Just pick up after he does his doody..." he snickered at his humor, "Doody. Get it?"

I chuckled. "Yeah, I do."

"Well, let's see the furry beast!"

Tina had her window cracked and heard that so she spoke softly to Opus, giving him a command I couldn't hear and opened her door. She left it open, the dome light illuminating the growing darkness. She walked over to my side and put her arm around me in a one-sided hug and whistled softly. Opus hopped out and walked over, pushing his way in between us and then sat, his tongue hanging out the side of his mouth.

"Who's this all?" The old man asked.

"This is my fiancé Tina, and the fur ball that owns us is named Opus," I answered after hesitating to see if Tina was going to speak first, "And I'm Rick," I told him, walking forward and holding out my hand.

He took it. "I'm Charles, Charlie to my friends—"

A shrill bark sounded from behind him, and he turned to look. "Is Opus dog-aggressive?"

"*Sitz, blieb,*" Tina commanded, and Opus's wagging tail stopped, and he looked up at her, his head cocked to the side.

"He'll stay like that until she lets him go," I told Charles.

Another bark and Charles held up a finger to indicate a moment, and he turned, his hand on the railing and went up to his door and opened it. A toy poodle bounded out. The dog was probably no more than five pounds soaking wet and had the energy of a squirrel that was overdosing on crack and caffeine, at the same time.

"Fifi, nice dog!" Charles commanded as the small animal charged Opus, barking, and growling.

I was worried, and I almost called off Fifi when I saw her coming, but Opus just looked at Tina, and then me, to ask if he really had to endure the scolding from the tiny dog.

"*Platz*," Tina said in a soft voice, and Opus lay down, putting his paws out in front of him.

Fifi darted in, and before I could warn or stop it, she licked Opus in the face. He took it like a champ, turning his head before he licked the other dog back. That, in turn, prompted the little dog to go behind him, and as Tina and I turned to watch what Fifi was doing, I heard Charles chuckle.

"Now she's gonna try to hump him, I guess," I whispered.

"I don't think it works like—"

"*Shhhh*," Tina scolded.

Fifi took a quick sniff and then ran back up to Opus, spun around in a circle and Opus got his own sniff in and then Fifi played gently, Opus finally raising a paw to push the small dog back.

"He's a good one. Gentle," Charles said. "Tell you what, go ahead and set up at 198, it's the last slot on the left. There's nobody right on ya, so if your dog is startled in the middle of the night, it won't wake no one up. I figure you want to use the showers and bathhouse?"

"That would be great," I admitted.

He nodded and fished out a key and tossed it to me. "Leave a twenty in the door jamb before you pull out, though I might be awake."

"Thank you," I said, knowing he was giving us a deep discount.

"No problem. You get some rest now, it's time for me to watch another episode of Game of Thrones. Fifi, come on."

He turned to walk back, as both Tina and I called thank you in soft voices. After a moment, Fifi gave up the game and hurried in, where Charles was holding the door open patiently for her.

"You ready to camp?" Tina asked.

"Sounds good to me," I said, as my back gave me a warning twinge that I'd overdone it.

"You coming, buddy?" I asked fur face as I turned and heading back to the van.

I opened the door but he was still sitting on the ground next to a grinning Tina, her features almost lost in the dark. She gave a soft command, and he bounced to his feet and let out a soft *woof* and bounded into Tina's side. I smiled and got in and waited for her. Wise to his tricks, Tina told him to get in his spot before she climbed up. Then, we headed off to find the spot Charles had told us about.

———

THE LYRICS TO THE SONG KEPT PLAYING OVER AND OVER. Somebody's watching me. I knew it, I was being chased and then—

A light clicked on, and Opus began licking my face in earnest. I pushed him back and saw that Tina had turned on the electric lantern I had used when we'd set up the air mattress.

"You were having a bad dream. I couldn't wake you up," she said sleepily, rolling to her side.

"I'm sorry," I told her, my heart thumping hard.

"You shouldn't be. I had to wake Opus up to wake up you. Good boy," she finished in a baby voice, and I could hear Opus's tail start thumping, "You want to tell me what it was about?" she asked.

"That damned video on my computer. I was being chased. It's... I don't really remember it," I said, rolling onto my back, running my hands through my hair.

"Hey, it's a road trip, you're outside your normal cave, you just moved in with your lady love... and... you're about to meet *the parents*."

I snickered. "How many movie references did you just squeeze into a sentence?" I asked her.

"A lot," she whispered sleepily and turned off the light.

She murmured something else, but I was already closing my eyes as she curled into my right side tightly, her body warm against mine. I was drifting off when I felt more movement, and Opus settled on my left. I opened one eye to see him lying on his paws, his head near my face. He licked my nose, but I was so tired, I didn't even—

———

CHARLES AND FIFI WERE UP WHEN WE DROVE UP TO PAY, on our way out. The aroma of coffee could be smelled from a dozen paces, and I mentally vowed to find someplace that had decent coffee, because with a pang... I realized I hadn't packed any and left all of my favorite drug of choice in the motorhome.

"Come on in," Charles hollered as I attempted to sneak the twenty dollar bill into his doorway.

I hesitated, then pulled it all the way open. The fifth wheel opened up into a salon, with the table on one side across from me and a sink on the left. To the right of that was a small Lazyboy that looked like it was mounted on a swivel near a doorway to what I would guess was a small bedroom.

"Hi, I just wanted to pay up before I hit the road," I told him, seeing him sitting at the table, drinking my drug of choice out of an insulated Yeti.

"No problem. You and the missus want to stay for breakfast?"

"I uh... I have a camp stove, one of those little folder things. I already cooked and cleaned up, but I appreciate it," I said trying not to look as he took a long pull of the dark, luxuriously smelling—

"Well, at least let me get you a cup for the road! Make sure you stop back in next time you're through this way."

"Thank you," I said and watched Charles hop up like he was thirty years younger. He reached into a cupboard to my left and pulled out a pack of Styrofoam cups and a pack of lids. He poured two cups, and put the tops on.

"Sorry, I don't have any cream and sugar, I don't drink it like that myself," he said.

"Thank you," I told him, "I appreciate it, especially letting us in so late at night."

"I don't sleep much none anyways," he said with a grin.

With that, I thanked him again and headed back to the van and got in, juggling the two steaming cups.

"Cream and sugar?" Tina asked.

"He was all out."

She pouted, and I chuckled.

"What?" she asked.

"More for me. I'll find you some as soon as I see some-place," I told her.

It didn't matter though, we'd both gotten six hours of sleep and a long, hot shower. It had done a lot to loosen the kinks in my back. Then I'd heated water, and we'd scarfed down some oatmeal before letting Opus loose and made sure he knew to be quiet and not to go chasing the squirrel terrorists... if there *were* any in Nebraska, because, for the most part, it was corn fields as far as the eye could see.

By the time I reached the highway, I heard soft snores. I looked over and saw Tina had fallen back asleep, her head near the seat belt strap, with Opus sitting, his head in her lap. He looked at me and then forward as if to tell me to hurry up, so I gave up on coffee and got back on the road. No matter how much sleep I needed, five or six hours was the most I got, so I wasn't upset that Tina didn't hold the same schedule I did. I'd let her sleep, and when she woke up, maybe we'd get some lunch. With the sun coming up, I mentally said goodbye to the KOA campground, and Nebraska in general, and drove with the rising sun in my rearview.

9

TINA

Staying awake was difficult for Tina and Opus. She didn't mind the long silences that happened when Rick got involved in his mental planning. She actually preferred it sometimes. Small talk wasn't her specialty as she was so direct, so it always felt awkward. Rick seemed to be comfortable with them as well, both of them comforted by each other's presence.

The thing she was having a lot of fun with, was running Rick's Facebook account while he was driving. People she'd never seen before nor heard of were commenting, liking and sharing the posts and pictures of what they had been doing. It made her proud that, in her own way, she was supporting him in his dreams. He was often hard on himself and a little insecure, but she thought that was a common writer trait.

Opus made a grunt and Tina looked over to see the big fuzzy-headed pup put his head down, then get to his feet and turn a circle before curling up between Tina and Rick. The bump between the seats from the dash radiated heat, and with the air conditioning cranked, Opus was finding his own area where he could keep himself as warm as he wanted.

"What do you think, buddy?" Rick asked, his eyes barely leaving the road.

Opus snored softly between them.

"I think he's going to sleep a lot on this trip," Tina said, playing with her phone, chatting with his Virtual Assistant through Facebook Messenger.

"Probably bored out of his fur," Rick said, then went quiet.

I love your idea

Thanks, I'd love to help. I think he's going to be surprised when he sees his fan's responses to this.

I think so, too. He's been a great sport on this and he's having fun, but he's not talking much.

Brooding?

Tina thought about that question then thumbed out her response.

Maybe a little bit. I caught him dictating and I think he's getting a little burned out. Either that, or the thought of meeting my father is getting to him.

Men are always afraid of meeting the parents. Something about shotgun weddings when the blushing bride turns up preggers before the question is asked...

Hush your mouth!!! LOL I am not preggers. Maybe someday. We haven't talked about that.

You should. He's told me... well, never mind. That was private. What we're doing is girl-talk.

That's not fair!

Tina was almost angry at that, but she understood.

I know, I know, but he pays my salary :)

No, I get it. He's kicking around the idea of writing in a new genre. Has he talked to you about it?

NO

Oh well, nothing like letting the cat out of the bag, lol.

Let me know when you know!

I will, girl. Let's keep our talk a secret for a few more days. I want to see his face when he knows I've been helping in the background.

I don't understand why he doesn't know already.

I want to surprise him. The both of us are so... self-contained? I'd like to give him a nice surprise.

It will be! When you show him the fan club you set up for his reader ladies...

Gotta run, we're pulling into a gas station. I need coffee!

Laters!

"You want some coffee?"

"I'd love some coffee. The drive is so relaxing I might fall asleep without the caffeine."

Opus stirred between them, then stood and stretched.

"Have a good nap, boy?" Rick asked.

"Of course he did, he's a growing boy," Tina cooed.

Opus rumbled low in his throat, not threatening, but letting her know that it wasn't quite bullshit.

"Want me to take him for a walk?" Rick asked.

"That would be awesome," Tina told him. "God, I love you."

"Do you hear that Opus? She loves me. I wonder if she knows how much I love her?"

Tina had been getting out when she heard that, her eyes going wide.

"You still scared of saying it?"

Opus hopped out Rick's side and Tina slammed her door, waiting near the front of the big van.

"She thinks I'm scared of telling her I love her," Rick told Opus.

Tina made a low growling sound in her throat, not unlike Opus, a sign of her light frustration, and stomped off to get caffeine.

Lots of caffeine.

RICK

I 'd seen mountains before.

In books, magazines and even on TV. I was not prepared to see them in real life like I thought I was. Not only was the air a little thinner when I caught my first glimpse, but it felt like the rest of my breath had been sucked out of my mouth. I put my blinker on and slowed down in the breakdown lane. I pulled to a stop and felt a wet nose push up against my hand. I pet my fuzzy buddy and opened the door. Tina had fallen asleep again after lunch, and I'd worked on dictating an outline for a story in a different genre.

I wasn't going to abandon what I was doing, but Tina's suggestion had given me an idea to do something outside of the normal. I walked around to the side door, not having let Opus out on the driver's side. I could tell by the way he wiggled that he wanted out to stretch and to mark a tree... well, in this case, a rock or shrub. The breakdown lane here almost looked like an uphill runaway lane and had two empty lanes of traffic beside it. I'd pulled off onto the gravel edge of the shoulder.

"Come on boy, you gotta go?" I asked him. He bounded out.

"Whazzat?" Tina said in a fuzzy voice, and then sat up suddenly.

"Hey, babe," I said reaching over the seat to touch her shoulder. "I just pulled off to let Opus go to the bathroom and take a picture.

Tina looked over her shoulder at me and then ahead of her. She cracked her door open and stepped out.

"You want me to take a picture of you with the snow caps in the background?" She rubbed her eyes.

"I uh... I was going to take a picture of the..."

"Stand over there," she said, smiling and pulling my phone from my hands and pointing to where I was supposed to go.

I listened, and Opus joined me a second later. "She's kind of pushy, isn't she?" I asked him.

He chuffed.

"I heard that, you two," Tina said, and then took a few pictures and waved me back over and handed me the phone.

"I didn't do it, can't prove it," I lied.

Opus hopped into the van, and disappeared into the middle, where he liked to sleep behind the bump that's called the doghouse.

"Wow, how long was I out?" Tina asked.

"Well, we have... I don't know... a couple hours left until the edge of Utah?" I pocketed my phone.

"You know, you don't have to let me sleep all the time."

"I know, but you didn't get any sleep last night."

"Neither of us did. You're driving though."

I had coffee! With that, I can conquer all!

"We'll stop earlier," I told her. "Maybe we should go somewhere that we can do a sit-down dinner."

"It's up to you." She grinned and wrapped the front of me with both arms, pulling me close in a hug.

"Well, we're just about there, and we're early for the show so I guess we can take it slow from here on out?"

Her answer was a kiss, and after that, I was definitely looking to stop sooner than later. The hotel we found wasn't a chain, just a mom and pop setup that looked like old log cabins had been built right next to each other. I paid for the night, and then we walked next door to the restaurant and bar, Opus following us.

"I'm going to go in and ask if they mind. Some places are—"

"Hey there," a man said, coming out the door, a little unsteady on his feet.

"Hi," Tina and I chorused, and stepped out of the way, watching him head toward the hotel and thankfully not one of the cars parked next to the bar.

"I can, if you want me to, I will," I told her, hearing a jukebox playing an old western song.

She smiled and made a shooing gesture. I took the hint and went inside.

The bar was built like the small cabin motel next door. Old logs, worn smooth from countless hands, made the outer walls. There were a couple dozen tables on one side, where the other was a little more open. A pool table dominated one open area, a dart board and a taped off area in another. People seemed to be mostly congregating near the bar or the pool table though. There were stuffed mounts, boar, deer, elk and even a moose hanging at various corners, but the moose is what caught my eye. The enormous rack of the creature had been adorned with various bras hanging from it. I did a double take to see that the rack was holding up something that usually held up—

"How many, or do you want to sit at the bar?" a woman in a red checkered shirt, tied at the waist above skin-tight jeans asked, her hair a mass of black curls held down by a straw cowboy hat.

"My fiancé and me. But I was wondering, is it dog-friendly in here?"

"Service animal?" she asked, a smile tugging at the corner of her lips.

"Well, he's a protection dog. I don't know if she's actually gotten the—"

"Oh yeah, working dogs like that are allowed in this place, especially if they're well-behaved," she said, and then ducked as something sailed over her head.

I saw it out of the corner of my eye; a bald man who looked remarkably like the woman I was talking to was smirking as he pulled another cardboard coaster out.

"Daddy, stop!"

"Is your pooch well-behaved?" he asked, giving me a grin.

"Yes. We just don't want to leave him in the van while we eat and he'll stay under the table, no worries."

"Well, tell your missus and your fuzzy friend to head on in. I'll get you menus," he said, and got up and headed toward the bar.

I went out and motioned for Tina, a smile on my face.

I'd missed something in that exchange. Something the father had picked up on or that had been going on before we went in. I puzzled that as Tina put her hand into mine and we headed over to the table that the waitress was waving me over to.

I pulled Tina's chair out, and she smiled up at me as she sat, then I took my spot. Since the table wasn't as large as I'd hoped, only big enough for four chairs pushed halfway in, Opus sat on the outside, between Tina and me.

We ordered drinks; me the kind that could do serious damage if I had more than two, and then looked over the menu.

"You hungry, buddy?" Tina asked him.

"I bet you he wants a bacon cheeseburger, minus the bun," I told her.

Opus whined.

"Or, some bacon cheese fries with a side of smoked sausage and some—"

Opus whined louder and got up, putting his head on his mom's lap, his tail wagging.

"My daughter wanted to know if you'd sign this?" the dad said, coming back out, a book in one hand, a tray of ice water in another.

I looked up and saw his name tag as well. Curtis. He was holding one of my newer PNR books, my face clearly on the back cover. I had been embarrassed about doing that, but my cover designer and my VA both talked me into it. Apparently, it was 'my brand.' I'd run into people that had heard of me, but this was the first time somebody had recognized me by sight, that I could recall.

"Sure," I said and took the book and the pen, then opened the cover. "I uh... missed her name," I admitted.

"Jessica," he said with a grin, giving me the nonverbal that he was doing this for his daughter and it amused him that she had sent him out and not come out herself.

"Here you go," I said, handing him the book back.

"Thanks. She'll be out soon, I hope," he chuckled and headed toward the bar where he'd been sitting earlier.

"What was that about?" Tina asked me, a wry grin on her face.

"I think... you know what, it'd only be a guess at this point," I admitted.

After a couple minutes, I was expecting Curtis to bring our drinks, but a red-faced Jessica came out and gave us our daily ration of alcohol and thanked me for signing her book. I told her no problem, and we put in our orders. Two patties for Opus with bacon and cheese, I went for a chicken sandwich, and Tina got herself a chicken Caesars salad. Jessica wrote it all down and then headed back toward the bar, where I assumed the kitchen was behind the narrow door.

"So, you have a fan...?" Tina teased.

"I guess so," I told her. "First time that's happened."

"No, it isn't!" she said. "Annette remembered, you told me about that."

"Annette knew my name. She," I pointed toward the small swinging door, "recognized me from the book. I always thought it was a mistake to put that picture on there."

"You're just self-conscious," Tina said, scooting her chair toward me a little bit, making Opus look up at her sharply as her chair squeaked.

She took my hand.

"It's weird," I told her in a quiet voice.

"It's only weird if you make it weird. Wait, what are you talking about exactly; that you have a fangirl, or that you have your picture on a book jacket?"

"Both," I admitted.

"*Oooohhhhh*," she said and poked me in the side as I was trying to take a drink of my rum and coke.

It went down the wrong pipe, and I barely turned my head as I coughed, setting my drink down. Tina laughed for a moment, then pounded my back, and a wet tongue got the bottom of my chin. My eyes watered with the rum seemingly coming out of my nose and I sat up, giving Opus a pat on the head and grabbed a napkin and wiped my face as the wracking coughs subsided. I hoped the fur face had a good laugh, Tina sure did.

"Your timing sucks," I told her.

"I'm sorry," she said with a grin.

I wiped my face and the table in case I'd made more of a mess than I'd seen before, and made sure my eyes weren't watering from the strong spirits. I usually stuck to beer, but for some reason, I'd felt like ordering a Manhattan.

That was when our food came out. Jessica dropped it off, thanked me again for signing her book and took off to drop off her tray and reload with food for another table. A jukebox played an old country song, and I took a sip of my drink, letting the booze relax me, and the tension left me.

"Ma'am, can I ask you to dance?" a man asked.

"Well, I don't..." Tina's words trailed off.

The man looked to be about old Sarge's age. He was

wearing denim from head to foot with the exception of a black felt Stetson, and he carried a black lacquered cane. Tina looked at me, and I smiled and shrugged.

"Sure," she said to the man, while standing up.

They made their way to an open spot between the tables. The old cowboy leaned his cane against a chair, and they danced slowly. Opus stood up and looked at them, then at me.

"He's harmless, buddy. If it was one of the younger guys, I might have had an issue. Probably going to make the old man's night, her dancing with him. Don't you think?"

He chuffed and then sat up straighter as he noticed the food I hadn't shared out yet. I took one of the smaller plates and cut the bacon cheeseburger (minus the bun) into three strips, grease filling the bottom of the plate as the burger had been cooked to perfection.

Opus whined, and I set the plate down near my foot. Ten seconds later it was completely gone, and Opus was licking his chops. I set Tina's ice water down and held the edge as he lapped water out. When we got into the hotel room, I'd get out his food and water dishes. Right now was just a special treat. Opus was on the larger size for his breed, and he could easily have eaten four burgers, but all the grease would have made him gassy later on. I'd found that out the hard way.

"Thank you," Tina said as the old cowboy was pulling her chair back out.

The song hadn't been a long one and judging by the limp, even that much dancing had taken its toll on the cowboy.

"Thank you for letting me take your lady for a twirl,"

he told me, one hand resting on the table heavily, on my left side.

"It's no problem. You want to sit a minute, rest your leg?" I asked, noting that it was his left leg that he was almost dragging.

"If you don't mind, that'd be great."

Opus looked up over the table as the cowboy almost fell into the chair, and they started at each other for a long moment. "And what's your name, fella? A big guy like you should be a Brutus or Zeus... or, I know, maybe it's Bocephus?"

"That's my baby, Opus," Tina said with a grin.

Right then and there I decided that, despite being the world's most introverted introvert, I was going to learn how to dance because I could see that Tina's color was up and her smile touched her eyes. Opus put his head in her lap, a welcome back hug.

"Looks half-wolf to me. I'm Oscar."

"Rick," I said offering my hand, which he shook promptly, "You know my Tina already, and our fuzzy son, Opus."

"You don't own no dog. The dog owns you!" Oscar said, and Opus chuffed at him in response.

Tina and I laughed, and I slid my plate in his direction. "Hungry?"

"No sir, just saw a pretty lady. Miss Tina, please know this isn't a line, but you do look an awful lot like my daughter. I do appreciate you giving me the honor of a dance."

"It was my pleasure," she said, noticing her water glass was half empty, and she shot me the stink eye.

I pulled my plate back and dug in. Opus went from

Tina over to me, laying his head on my leg, totally shameless. I handed a fry down as Oscar the cowboy watched.

"Where is your daughter?" Tina asked, not letting the silence get awkward.

"Fallujah," he said, looking at her again, fighting a smile.

Tina turned up the wattage, and he grinned. So cheesy, but as soon as he smiled, she picked up her burger, almost the size of her head, and took a big bite.

"Army?" I asked for lack of a better question.

"Yeah, she's attached to a helicopter. Door gunner and electronics specialist. I worried about her for years and years, but she says it's important work and she's in no more danger than anybody else over there. Probably less, truth be told."

"That's good," I said watching as Tina's eyes almost rolled into the back of her head, the burgers were that good.

"Anyways, I think I'm a little steadier on my feet. Even though you kinda look like my little Danielle, I did appreciate the dance from a pretty lady," he said then tipped his hat her way and got to his feet slowly, leaning on the cane.

"Thank you for the dance. That was fun."

He gave us both a grin and pointed at Opus, then Tina, and some silent communication passed between the three of them, and Opus let out a chuff. I thought I had an idea what went on, but I could only say what I'd have thought of it. He was telling fur face to keep an eye on his momma. I gave him a polite wave, and he gave me one back.

Tina watched him go for a second and then dug into

her burger. I'm not the world's largest man, but compared to Tina, I was probably double her. She polished off her food faster than I could finish mine, and I gave half of my fries to Opus.

She had one sip of my drink, coughed and then finished down her Sprite. Feeling full and relaxed, I paid my tab for the food and drink and then made my way back to the table where Opus was standing up, the fur on his back at attention on the ridge over his spine. A low growl emanated, but it was too low to hear over the thump of the music coming out of the jukebox. Two men were standing behind Tina, who'd turned to one side to talk to one of them.

"See, my husband is a real person," she said, showing me an exasperated look.

"That ain't no husband. Neither of y'all are wearing a ring," he said, clearly inebriated and swaying, but definitely not in tune with the music.

"I told you, Steve, let's go. The lady doesn't want to dance," the less drunk of the two said, pulling on the shoulder of the man who'd been talking to Tina.

He was about my height, but wiry. I probably had a good twenty or thirty pounds on the guy, most of it in the upper body. He looked like if he stood up straight, he'd droop, but I could see the scars across his fists and a few on his face. He'd been a scrapper, probably still was. Opus increased his volume, teeth starting to show.

"Nein," I whispered, and he broke eye contact with the man and looked at me. "These two were just going now, weren't they?" I finished, but I was looking at the less drunk friend.

"Yeah, we're going to get going," he said tugging on his friend's shoulder again.

He shrugged the grip off and shot him a look. "If she can have a dance with that crusty old cowpoke, then she can take time out of her precious day to have a dance with me."

He turned to Tina. "Right, sweetheart?"

Jessica walked out of the batwing doors separating the kitchen from the bar and saw the tension from both me and Opus. She ducked back behind the door.

"I'm not dancing with you," Tina said, not standing up. "So, you might as well go."

"I told you, honey—" he started to say, but as soon as he tried to grab her shoulder Opus launched himself over the table.

He didn't latch on with his teeth, but the bulk of over one hundred pounds of canine hitting him in the chest while he was already tipsy was all it took. I was already moving, and Tina was giving him the command to break off, stand down. The German command she gave was almost lost over the chorus of a song about some punk who cheated on his wife and how she keyed the crap out of his truck. I ignored all of that and got between Tina and the two men, seeing Opus had two feet on the ground, two feet on the man's chest, snarling a warning.

"Opus, I got—"

A knife flashed from the man's right hand, and Opus jumped back. I'd pulled my Beretta out in a smooth motion just as Tina was screaming for everyone to stop. The man with the knife saw me draw and he held still, the knife in his fist, still over his chest.

"Opus, back down, I got this," I said, my voice as

much of a growl as the dog's had been as I clicked off the safety.

"Mister, I'll be getting," the less drunk friend said and began backing away, his hands in the air.

The shouting had drawn attention, and somebody decided at that point to pull the power cord on the juke-box. The entire bar turned to stare at us from what I could see in my peripheral vision. I kept my eyes trained on the drunk's face, watching for his hand to move.

"Rick, easy," Tina said from behind me.

"Put the knife down," I told him.

"Your dog's crazy, man. He attacked me. All I wanted was a dance."

I wanted to put a bullet in the floor, next to his head, between his legs. Something awesome and dramatic, but instead I lowered the gun and held it lower, more or less in the direction of the man's groin. He noticed and dropped the knife and covered up his crotch.

"I don't want no more trouble," he said.

"My wife's dog has been perfectly trained to protect her. She told you to leave, and you put your hands on her. He very gently made you get back, but let me tell you something, he could have easily torn your throat out. He didn't. He is not crazy, he was very deliberate and calcu-lated with his violence. Just like I will be, if I need to. Now, are we going to have a problem?" My words were low, but I had a feeling everyone in the bar could hear me.

He just stared at me, not saying anything, both hands held over his crotch. For drama, I pulled the hammer back, the action the loudest thing in the room.

"No problem, I'm sorry I tried to knife your dog," he said in a blubbering voice.

I put the hammer down, made the pistol safe and then holstered it under my shirt. I took a step toward him, and he flinched, but I was holding out my hand while stepping on his knife with my left shoe. After a second, he took it, and I helped him to his feet. Tina was beet red, very angry, but she was standing on the other side of the table from me, whispering commands or comfort to Opus, I couldn't tell which.

"Get out of here, Dewayne," Jessica said, a double barrel shotgun resting easy in her arms, held at the low and ready.

That surprised me, but I guess it made sense that the bar had a gun behind it, I'd just thought a double barrel behind the bar was a cliché that writers used. This time, it was the truth.

"Yes ma'am," the drunk said and scrambled to his feet.

We all watched as he shuffled out of the bar, and a few moments later his less drunk friend paused at the doorway. "Sorry about that, he normally ain't like this."

"Just go," Jessica's dad called from the table near the bar where he'd been sitting.

He got gone. Adrenaline let down made me suddenly feel like my legs were made of rubber. I was about to sit down when Tina made a sound.

"What?" I asked her.

"Go wash your hands," she said, smiling despite still being upset.

"Huh?" I asked her, leaning down to pick up the knife the drunk had dropped and set it on the table.

"He peed his pants, that's why he covered his crotch, and you helped him up."

I looked at my hands and then back at her. She pointed at Opus to tell me she had everything five by five so I shrugged and went to the bathroom and washed my hands thoroughly. As I was coming out, somebody clapped, and then the room erupted in laughter and talk. I walked back to the table where I'd left Tina and Opus. Tina was laughing, and I saw her put her hand on Jessica's shoulder, both ladies cackling. Opus was sitting at attention, but his tongue was hanging out the side of his mouth as he breathed fast. He was smiling and lapping up the attention.

"Hey, I had to call the cops," Jessica's dad, Curtis informed me.

"Well..." I said and sat down.

"Don't worry, you have a whole bar full of witnesses. He's a local, so you did us a favor. He won't be coming around here no more, not with yellow streaks coming down his pants. Damn, I have to mop the floor now."

The crowd roared laughter and Tina caught my eye while she was talking with Jessica, she dropped me a wink and made a head bob motion toward the exit. Oh yeah. I was ready to go too.

"Curtis, we're staying next door, the third cabin down. If they want to talk to me, that's fine. I've had a long day though."

"Good enough. I'll let them know."

Jessica hugged Tina hard and whispered something else to her, and both ladies giggled and said their good-byes. I waited until Opus and Tina made it to my side.

"The cops might not want to talk to us after all," she whispered to me as we headed outside.

"Oh yeah?" I asked her.

"Jessica's boyfriend is a cop," she giggled.

Uh, then why was she...? That's when I realized that what little I understood about the female gender was not even half as much as I thought I knew. What had really been going on in there? I had no idea. I'd ask Tina about it later, but I was still coming down from my adrenaline dump. I opened the door to our motel room and flopped face first on the bed, letting my feet hang off the end. Opus let out a low *woof* sound and hopped up next to me. The last thing I remember, was Tina crawling on the bed, straddling my waist as she worked the knots out of my lower back, then my shoulders. Then—

11

TINA

Tina knew that Rick carried all of his tension between his shoulder blades, and when he flopped face-first on the bed, he was at his limit. It had been a dicey situation. She'd been terrified of the pushy drunk, Dewayne, until she'd seen Rick walking back to their table. When she saw that, she knew he could disarm the situation without having to force Opus to act.

He was her protective dog, had bonded with her on a level that was so deep that, in both of their minds, they were family. One of her biggest long-term fears was that the darkness would find her again and Opus would defend her... Then Opus would pay the price because many people didn't value the life and care of companions like him the way she did.

If he attacked somebody and was found at fault, even if defending her, they could take him away and it was usually a short walk that ended with a needle. She didn't want that. So, when Rick had come out, she'd been suddenly relieved. He could handle it, and he did.

He and Opus had moved like a team, just like they had with the guy who had tried to rob her last year. It was like these two instinctively knew how the other was going to react and moved together, as a unit. Opus had never, ever trusted somebody on sight like he did Rick, and she was thankful for the day she decided to put a lot of trust in his instincts; lord knows she had a horrible track record herself.

She straddled Rick's back, slowly kneading the muscles, starting at his waist and slowly moving up, using her palms and fingers to knead his flesh from the spine out. Opus jumped up on the second bed, but his head perked up when he heard Rick let out a little groan as the tension left his body.

Soon, Rick was snoring softly, his feet hanging off the end of the bed.

"Oh great," Tina griped, and Opus looked at her, his head between his paws.

"He can't sleep in his shoes and clothes. Want to help me?"

Opus remained silent, but his big eyes stared at her with love and kindness.

Tina removed his shoes and tried to roll him over. He snored louder and she decided that with him weighing almost a hundred pounds more than her, she'd just strip the blanket from the other bed and cover him up. She briefly thought about sleeping on the other bed, but she knew if she did, the dream might come back.

In the nights they'd spent together, the dream had almost gone away entirely. Before they had moved in together, it had been a nightly occurrence. It had been coming less and less and now that they were rarely apart.

That was only a side benefit of having Opus and Rick around. Truth was, she loved him so much it hurt and she didn't want to scare him with how vulnerable she'd felt before he'd come into her life.

THE BATHROOM DOOR WAS CLOSED. SHE RUSHED FROM THE kitchen to the bathroom and slammed and locked the door. Despite the restraining order, she was sure she'd just seen Lance's Oldsmobile parked exactly one hundred yards from the mini-storage.

In the darkness, she hadn't been able to tell if he was in it. She'd called the cops on him twice before for the same thing, but the police had told her that he wasn't breaking the restraining order and there was nothing they could do, except talk to him. The second time a detective had gone out and parked behind him, talking to him. Lance made up some lie about bird watching. There was nothing to hold him on, so they let it go, warning him not to follow Tina.

Tonight, he was back, and she didn't want to call a fourth time. The third time they had told her there was nothing she could do. Tina splashed cold water on her face and felt nauseous. More than once she had considered getting a gun. She could shoot, but she was thinking a pistol, something she didn't have.

Tonight, she'd get the shotgun out from under the bed and load it and pray she wouldn't need it. Next, she'd Google dog breeders. She wanted something big, mean, and loyal. She had happened to stumble across a Facebook ad about a local breeder of German Shepherds. She'd have to do the training with the puppy, but—

The sound came from the bedroom. The thump was felt through the wall on which she'd placed one hand to brace herself, while she looked at her reflection in the mirror. Thump. Something sounded like it scraped across the closet door on the wall on the other side of the mirror.

Dread filling her, she opened the bathroom door, ready to bolt—

"You're having a bad dream," Rick said, pulling her close, his breath hot on the back of her neck.

Still sleepy, but understanding she'd escaped the dream in time, she let out a shuddering breath and let Rick's warmth and love wrap her up; protective, comforting.

It wasn't long thereafter, her snores matched pace with Rick's.

12

RICK

The policeman took my statement as I was checking out. What happened, what did I do, and who did I do it to. The dog didn't bite anybody, and that was that. I signed my name, and the entire process was finished as the receptionist at the motel printed out a receipt for me. I felt amazing, and we were only a couple hours away from our destination with most of the day ahead of us. That was how we found ourselves loading up when Tina noticed her front tire was low.

"Hey hon, my tire's half flat," she told me.

I cursed quietly. My spare was on the front of the van, and I hadn't replaced the tire yet. My spare was actually a full size tire mounted on a rim the exact size as my other tires. If this tire blew... I headed back inside the motel and got directions to the closest tire shop. Walking back out, I was mentally planning out my trip. The tire was low, but it didn't look half flat. I smiled, knowing that I could limp the van along instead of calling AAA.

"What's got you smiling like a cat that ate the canary?" Tina asked me as I fired up the van.

"We can get the van to the tire shop, we won't have to call for a tow truck," I told her.

"Your grin is bigger than that," Tina teased.

"Last night," I admitted.

"What, the whole knight in shining armor, making a known troublemaker so scared he peed his pants? For scaring off a knife-wielding rapscallion?"

"I was going for the whole massage that turned into you falling asleep on top of Opus and me, but that other stuff too," I said, and put the van in gear as she made a happy sound.

More had happened, but I'd had to wake up for that, and I had stayed awake for a while. We'd kicked the dog off the bed, and he'd gone to the other side of the room, guarding the front door.

We'd fallen asleep in a tangle as usual, and when I'd woken up in the morning, it was to the cold nose of Opus reminding me that he had to go outside. I didn't mention any of that though, but instead followed the directions I was given. Turn right on the service road, and it'd be two miles down on the right. I was going slowly, and I kept an eye on things. Hopefully, it was just a nail or something from the parking lot; it'd suck to have to replace two tires. It wasn't like a car tire, these were heavier duty truck tires. The lugs had to be put on tighter, the air pressure higher.

"There it is," Tina said, adding Captain Obvious to the mental list of nicknames I wanted to say.

"Thanks," I said, and put my blinker on.

I checked my rearview mirror and saw that the two times I'd pulled off the side of the road to let normal traffic pass had worked and I didn't have a big lineup behind me now. Just an old blue Astro van, but they were still a ways back. I pulled in, and one of the three overhead doors in front of the shop rolled up automatically, with a young man barely out of high school motioning me to drive straight in.

"Opus, you be good," I told him, not knowing how he'd react to parking inside a commercial building.

"He'll keep his cool, will you?"

"Of course," I snarked, smiling.

"What'll it be? Oil change? Fix a flat?" The young man asked from my side as I rolled down the window.

"That tire went low on me overnight. I have another one that blew out on my trip out here."

"Long trip?" he asked, seeing my Michigan parks tag on the windshield.

"Yeah, headed to Salt Lake City," I told him, "So might as well throw in an oil change, too."

"No problem. If you folks would like to wait in the office, I'll pull this tire off and get going on the oil change and get you some prices for that spare tire."

"Sounds good," Tina said from the passenger side, "I've got my dog with me, can I let him out to run in the grass a little bit?"

"Isn't much grass, ma'am, but he's welcome to do whatever he needs to do," the man said looking at Tina, turning red in the ears.

"Thank you," Tina said and crawled past me to exit out the side door.

She clipped a leash on Opus and was opening the door when I got out.

"I left the keys in it. You have a TV with the news I can turn on a little while?"

"Oh, sure," Stan said, now that I could see his name-tag.

"Thanks," I told him and walked toward the side door where the waiting area was.

It had half a dozen chairs, with a countertop where the cash register rested. A TV remote sat on one of the chairs, and the local news was on. I turned it up when Tina turned to me. "I'm going to let Opus run a little bit, do you want to come with us?"

Opus chuffed, as if to say he knew I needed a run, too. Since I felt like I didn't because running to run was a thing that only the new-me did and I'd had a couple days away from it...

"No, thanks. I want to catch the news. The Antifa protests have been all over the place lately, and I want to see if there are any problems—"

She interrupted my words with a kiss. Opus whined and then made a frustrated sound and got up on his hind legs, putting a paw on each of us and barked happily.

"Jealous much?" I asked him, and was rewarded with a lick on the face.

"Dog slobber," I said wiping at my face, hamming it up a bit as the dog got back down on all fours.

Opus barked happily, and Tina pushed herself away from me playfully. "We going to get a hotel room tonight?"

"It's up to you."

"I'm feeling like a slug for not working out the last couple of days. I am going to take Opus for some laps around here. I just don't want to go to bed all sweaty."

"What if I—"

"That's not what I said," she told me, and flicked the tip of my nose.

"I'll get a room. Maybe two, with a door in the middle."

Opus sneezed at me, more or less telling me my idea was bullshit, and he would take his own bed, or his own part of the bed, something he'd been doing off and on since we'd been together. Tina gave me a little wave and went out with Opus. I waved back and sat down and turned up the volume on the TV.

"...writer of Paranormal Fiction. The incident started when his wife was approached by an inebriated man. Their protection dog got involved in the altercation, and the suspect pulled a knife. In true western fashion, the pen-monkey drew his sidearm and held the suspect until the weapon was released before paying their tab and leaving."

I saw Jessica on the screen, holding up the book I signed for her. "It was over in a flash. I don't know who moved faster, the man or the dog. In all, it could have been an ugly situation. Weapons and booze don't mix, but everyone left the restaurant last night in an upright fashion."

I felt my cheeks burn hearing the story. I had just left a little while ago, and the news was there live. I was lucky.

"Just goes to show you, sometimes all it takes is a good guy with a gun to stop a bad guy with a gun," Jessica finished before the news segued into a weather report.

I saw a flash and realized it was Tina and Opus running past the windows, doing their first lap.

"Nothing wrong with that tire that's low," Stan said

coming in the door, but his eyes were on the jogging form of the other two members in my small family. "Probably got something wedged in the stem and let out a little bit of air. Your second tire is beyond saving. Looks like it punctured, and then shredded."

"Yeah, it blew out on the highway," I said, as he finally turned to face me. "I put the spare on."

"Was the tire that's low the spare tire you put on?"

"No, it was the rear right," I told him.

"Okay. I have one of those in stock. It's $279 for the tire and $45.99 for a full-service oil change."

"That's fine," I told him. "As long as you take a card?"

"Oh yeah," he said, wiping his hands on a rag. "When you get one or two customers a day, it doesn't pay to not take every form of payment."

That was when I realized that he was the only one there. Nobody was there at the register, and no one else was inside the shop area where my van was now lifted in the air.

"Slow?" I asked him.

"Not many people around here. Every six months or so, there's new miners, but after they get their junkers fixed up they drove in on, they don't do much driving until they're leaving the area. Not much business."

"Sorry to hear that," I told him truthfully, because I understood being in business for yourself, and sometimes it sucked.

"Naw, it works out for me. I make enough to keep the bills paid and me in beans, bullets, and Band-Aids."

I grinned real big when I heard that.

"Better to be a sheepdog—"

"Than one of the sheep," he finished with a chuckle,

looking me over again, before Tina and Opus running by caught both of our attention.

"Your wife?" he asked.

"Soon," I told him, watching as her hair bounced, one hand reaching up to pin her glasses back in place with Opus running circles around her slow jog. "I have to meet the parents and officially ask for permission."

"Congratulations, bro. Best be prepped to meet the dad."

"Prepped for about everything, I hope," I told him.

"Salt Lake City, you headed to PrepperCon?" he asked.

"Yeah? You going, too?" I asked, not surprised by this turn of events.

"I want to, but nobody to watch the shop. I hear there are going to be some fantastic bug-out RVs there."

"I saw that," I told him, thinking of the military vehicles that had been retrofitted and rebuilt to be every prepper's wet dream of RVs. "I've got an RV, but nothing as hardcore as those, that's one thing I want to see while I'm there, that and there are some authors I'd like to meet," I admitted.

"Yeah, I hear A. American is going to be there," Stan told me while he turned the clipboard around. On it was a filled-out estimate.

I signed it. "Me too. I'd like to get a couple books autographed," I admitted.

"Well, I'll get back at it," he said, as Tina went jogging past again.

I told him that was fine and headed outside. I could hear Tina and Opus's feet pounding the rocky ground as they made their way around the building. I waited and stretched some, feeling sore and, part of me, the part I usually ignore, wanted to join them in the run to loosen up my muscles. I shook my head at that thought, knowing this sudden health kick of mine was somewhat inspired by Tina and her influence.

"Going to join us?" she called as she came into sight.

"Not dressed for it," I told her as Opus gave me a playful bark as if to tell me to join in the run.

"Okay, one more lap for me," she said as she was almost around the building again.

I waited and looked out at the mountains. I don't know how high up we were, and honestly, I didn't know if we were still in Wyoming or part of Utah. The receipt for the hotel would tell me, but that was in the van. Still, I stretched some more, feeling the constrictive clothing I was wearing. Blue jeans, a T-shirt... real life clothing. Not like my daytime pajamas I was used to. Maybe I was changing? Engaged, ready to meet the parents and—

A gunshot crackled from a distance, the sound rolling over the hills. It sounded far off, probably somebody taking a potshot at a deer or elk, whatever they had out here.

That made me wonder if they were in season and after a moment, decided it didn't matter. I headed back inside as Tina and Opus rounded the corner again. I held the door open as she slowed down, but Opus went running in ahead of me, turning circles till Tina walked in, brushing her hair out of her eyes.

Surprisingly, she just wiped her forehead, and that was the extent of her warmup. I know she would probably walk around a little more to make sure she wasn't sore and properly cooled down, but she gave me a quick peck on the cheek and was watching the local news, that had looped the earlier footage.

"Did you know you and Opus made the local news?"

"I saw that," I said, feeling a little foolish to hear the story being played out. This would be another thing she'd use to poke fun at me.

"Good thing we left when we did. Sounds like this is the biggest thing to happen to this town in a while."

"Probably is," I admitted. "Looks like a sleepy little mining town with one bar, a gas station, and a general store." I flopped into a chair just as the report ended.

Tina sat on my leg and leaned back, wrapping her arm around me, pressing her cheek against mine, giving me a half hug. I squeezed her back till she made a wheezing sound and Opus was immediately there, his teeth pulling gently at the fabric of my shirt. I knew the pressure would increase till he was ripping, but as much as he was my buddy, I appreciated the fact he would go all out for Tina. I let her up, and she scooted over to get her own seat.

At least with us traveling, whoever had been trying to break into the mini-storage wouldn't worry her, nor the guy who'd got out of prison. If anything, I was more worried about what had happened with my Mac. Which reminded me... I got my cell phone out and navigated to the TeamViewer application and started the process of logging in remotely. The cell phone service here on top of the world seemed decent, but it took forever for my computer to connect. Once I logged in, I saw nothing had been messed with, and I let out a big sigh of relief.

"Everything okay?" Tina asked me distractedly, watching a news report on the TV.

"Yeah, was just checking on my computer. Nobody has left me any creepy YouTube videos up."

"Russians probably hacked you," Tina said, and I looked up at her, and she caught my gaze and laughed softly. "Gotcha!"

"Brat," I said under my breath, and Opus gave a chuff of agreement.

I checked on the files I'd uploaded that morning with the motel Wi-Fi. They were in my Dropbox folder like I thought they were. As soon as I fired up my SurfacePro, my new update with Dragon would see the files, automatically transcribe my recordings while on the road and then when I slowed down, I would edit and add the information to the manuscript. Last night had been a little too... lively. Opus had forgone the bed for a while and slept on his stomach, facing the door.

"Hey, that guy is fast," Tina said, and I looked up to see Stan walking our way, wiping a rag across his hands.

"Only one tire needed to be replaced. The spare," I told her as the glass door pushed open, Stan walking behind the counter.

"All set," he said, starting to punch things up on a computer and then looked at me. "Cash or charge?"

I was about to tell him charge when my cell phone rang.

"Charge," I mumbled pulling my wallet out of my pocket and hitting the answer button, wedged the phone on my shoulder to pull my wallet out.

"Hello?"

"...Congratulations, our records show that you've been selected to receive—"

I put my wallet on the counter and terminated the call.

"Telemarketer?"

"Worse," I muttered. "Scammer." I pulled out my card.

We said our goodbyes after paying him, and I pulled the van out and turned onto the service road. Opus didn't feel much like sleeping but instead gave me a soft bark, letting me know he was excited or happy about something. Tina immediately babbled in baby tongue to him and rubbed his ears. I found the on-ramp within moments and was accelerating up the grade. I could see the top, but it would take a little while to get there. One thing I noticed out west, the speed limits were crazy fast. There was no way I would feel comfortable going over 80 miles an hour in the wintertime with these mountain highways potentially iced.

The van's motor seemed to do well with the grades, and I watched the temperature gauge in some of the worst instances carefully and was doing so now, to make sure I didn't blow a gasket as the engine downshifted and the RPMs revved as we climbed, my speed slowly peeling away. Obviously, I wasn't the only one having an issue and put my blinker on to pass a blue van who was creeping up even slower than we were.

"We're going to be there soon, aren't we?" Tina asked.

"Yep."

"Give me your phone, it's time for you to do a Facebook Live event."

I groaned, but I fished the phone out of my pocket. I was glad I was wearing a hat today and had the lightweight zip-up camo hoody I used in the fall in Michigan.

I knew it would be cooler in the higher elevations and was glad I'd thought to pack it. Then again, I was going to lose it a couple states south as we moved through the desert and then into Arizona.

"You ready?" Tina asked, getting my phone ready to capture the right side of my face in profile.

In truth, my fans had loved the more human side of my Facebook interactions. After the news today, I worried that situation might go viral as well. Still, if it helped me sell more books...

"Yeah babe," I muttered, patting her on the leg.

13

RICK

Salt Lake City is breathtaking. It's a modern city built up in what looks like a valley, surrounded by mountains. On our way in, Tina pointed out some spots to pull off for pictures, but the closer I got, the more urgently I wanted to be there.

Even with all the delays and extra stops, we were still a day early. I knew I should have called ahead of time to reserve a hotel room, but figured I wouldn't worry about it too much. I found out the hard way that Utah is huge into prepping, and it's more than the large Mormon population. It was a way of life, and PrepperCon was pulling in vendors and customers from all points of the compass.

I ended up getting a room that wasn't labeled a suite, but it was a suite. Two beds, a built-in Jacuzzi tub in the middle of the room with a walkout patio with its own glass doors. It even had a kitchenette, a small apartment sized kitchen with everything needed to cook right here in the room. They hadn't even blinked about Opus, pointing out where the dog area was for when they were outside, and reminded us to pick up after our four-legged buddy.

"Oh, wow," Tina said turning around, taking in the view before running and flopping in the middle of the king-sized bed, the one near the patio windows.

"Yeah, this place comes with a great view," I said, and then under my breath, "It better have, with what they're charging for it."

"So how long do you want to stay?" Tina asked.

"I don't know," I told her. "I wanted to ask you. PrepperCon is going to be a two-day thing, maybe two and a half. We still have like eight days till we need to be in Arizona. I figure it's a ten to twelve-hour drive to your parent's house. Stay here for PrepperCon, maybe mosey down that way when we feel like it and see the sights?"

"I thought preppers were supposed to have plans? With backup plans to their plans and two is one and one is none, so you probably have three or four plans already. So, what is it?"

I hesitated for a moment or two. "Well, coming out this way was sort of your idea."

"So, you're going to blame your lack of planning on me?" she said, and pointed at me. "You've been wishy-washy. Whatever I want? What if I just want to spend time with you, doing something we will remember forever?"

"I like that plan," I told her, crawling on the bed and stopping near her.

I was amazed, a king-sized bed is *huge*. Like, it could easily fit both of us sleeping starfish style. Opus could take his portion anywhere, and there'd still be room for another dog. Hmm... That thought had me smiling, and Tina took that as an invitation and rolled my way. I pulled her in close. Opus, being the furry ball of jealousy and protectiveness, took that as an invitation to leave his post near the balcony's glass doors to come bounding across the room and jump on the bed. He pushed his snout between me and Tina, and gave us a kiss.

"Get off," Tina said, giggling and trying to cover her face.

"Opus, come on man. You're cutting in!" I admonished him, and he backed up, still standing on the bed, and sneezed at me.

"Ok, I know you're not really cutting in, but you interrupted something that might have been a lot of fun!"

He let out a soft bark, knowing not to go full volume inside hotels for some reason. I'd have to ask Tina about that now that I noticed it. Was it part of his training or was it something he learned in general? At the Mini Storage and the motorhome, he didn't have a volume control. My phone rang again. I looked at it this time, seeing that it was from the mini-storage.

"Hello?" I said like a brilliant conversationalist.

"Hey Rick, this is Char. Just checking in. How's my girl?"

"About to be ravished by a travel-weary stranger," I snapped, and choked back the laughter I almost let loose by the look on Tina's face.

"Uh, TMI kid... TMI. Hey, her phone's battery must be dead. I was just calling to say that Detective Stephenson arrested a young man and woman who were breaking into places in the area. He said that the man matches the description of the one who tried to break in here."

"That's good news," I told her, a weight lifting off my shoulders, "I'll let Tina know."

"Good. That girl never used to let her phone die all the time. I'm blaming it on you!"

"Bye, Char," I said.

"Later, Tater."

Tater?

"How're things?" Tina asked me, scooting as Opus finally decided to lay down, albeit in the middle of us.

"They arrested two people who were breaking into local places. One of them looks like it was the guy trying to get into the mini storage. Stephenson let Char know."

"Ohhhhh la la," Tina said batting her eyelashes.

"Yeah, but for a minute there I thought he was making a run at you," I admitted.

"Oh, you're the jealous type, are you?"

"You should know," I said leaning up over Opus and kissing her.

Opus put his paws over his snout and whined softly.

I WALKED AROUND WITH TINA FOR A WHILE, BUT I NEEDED to get some work done. I'd never left my dictation to sit for two or three days. If something went horribly wrong in the program, I'd have to re-listen to the recording to see what I was trying to say. That's why when Tina wanted to go for a jog, I told her I would stick behind. She took the mutt with her, so I took the opportunity to call downstairs and order a twenty-three dollar hamburger with fries and an eight dollar Budweiser. Having been poor so long, having money didn't really change the cheapskate in my soul, and I cringed at the price but confirmed I really wanted it and set up my computer at the snack bar, behind the small kitchenette and plugged in.

I got onto the Wi-Fi and was pleasantly surprised at the speed. Almost every hotel I'd ever been in had one Wi-Fi connection, and everybody was on it at once, and the speed was pretty horrible. A ton better than 4g, but still not great. This was great. In fact, it was almost as good as the internet I had upgraded at Tina's before I moved in. I hopped on Facebook a moment and saw there were over a dozen people who had messaged me earlier while I was driving and my notifications from the live stream were breaking the internet.

Most of it was fans congratulating me on an epic trip, or how they loved to see the pictures, a few were from old school friends. One was in Colorado and told me if I had a chance, stop in, and he'd show me some epic hills to climb. I checked out his Facebook page and saw that he'd taken up mountain climbing and had slimmed down quite a bit from how I remembered him in high school. I made a mental note because our journey out of the mountains might take me through parts of Colorado, or we could always backtrack two hours and go through the Mile High City then go south. We had days to burn, and Tina had made me understand she wanted me to have fun too, because she was.

I figured she just liked playing on my social media, but that detail I kept to myself. I finished looking at and commenting back on everything and then checked my emails. My VA had been doing more and more for me, and I saw a few things forwarded from her to my personal account that needed my attention, but it wasn't something I had to do right away, just for later in the month. I kept those and then wrote a note back to her when she asked me when I was going to get 'Bearly There' to her. That was what I was working on.

I was interrupted by the knock and went out and got my food, remembering at the last second to tip the guy who'd run the food up. I'd seen that in the movies, but I'd never really been one to live large, so I gave him a five, figuring that was probably appropriate for a thirty-dollar-ish meal. I took a swig of my beer and sat back down, dragging and dropping my recordings into the folder Dragon would use to auto-transcribe. It immediately went to work.

My phone pinged, and I picked it up. I'd closed Facebook on my computer, so the alert went there. It was another message from a fan or somebody random, and I was about to ignore it and dig into my burger when I decided to procrastinate a little bit longer.

Thinking that I thought of a little Yoda, chiding me, "Procrastinate much, work you will not finish." Yeah, I got it, but I was curious and unlocked the phone and opened the message, knowing I was going to mute it in a bit.

It wasn't somebody on my friend's list, it looked like a scammer profile. The picture was of a young woman, and I was almost ready to unleash my snark on her depending on her opening lines when I realized she'd sent two picture messages instead. One of them was of Tina, walking down a sidewalk, Opus happily following her. The second picture right under that was the one the

GEICO had commercial used for a while, with a more modern-day song. It was a stack of money, with eyeballs.

Somebody's watching me.

I shut down the app and thumbed Tina's name in and hit dial, fighting the urge to puke. Behind me, her phone rang. I cursed, remembering she'd turned it on after it got enough charge, but I hadn't realized she'd left the damn thing on the nightstand. I took a deep breath and then patted myself down. I had my newer Beretta, a 92fs, and it was smaller than the first one I had bought, so it was easier to conceal. Two magazines sat on the nightstand, and I grabbed those, my van keys, made sure I had the room key in my front pocket still, and stuffed it all in as I ran out. I barely hit my full speed when it was time to stop for the elevator, but I opted for the stairs instead.

Adrenaline fueled me in a way I didn't think it ever had before. I took great deep breaths and flew down the stairs. Nobody was on them, and it was a good thing because I think I skipped three or four in every flight on my mad dash down six flights of stairs. I had to remind myself to slow down, I was getting tunnel vision. I patted myself down to make sure I hadn't jostled anything loose as I got to the door leading to the lobby. I pushed the pocket knife in my left pocket down since it had ridden up as I ran and then took one more big, deep breath, and walked out into the hotel lobby.

The picture of Tina and Opus had a mountain in the background. Somebody was *here*.

The message... Was it a warning?

I didn't know which way to go, so I went outside and stood, looking around in the parking lot. A bark caught my attention, and I jogged around the corner toward the rear of a restaurant, almost missing the stunning back-drop of snow-capped mountains all around us.

Tina.

She was standing on the sidewalk, between two men who were walking toward her, a good twenty feet away from her on each side. I started that way, watching them and my hand itched as the man facing her pulled some-thing from his side.

Gun?

Was my first thought, but I was too surprised to act with the practiced hands of a gunslinger. Instead, the man facing her threw a frisbee easily over Tina's head toward his companion walking from the other direction.

"Get it," Tina called, and Opus took two running steps and leaped, catching it in his teeth, getting almost six feet of air.

I jogged over, feeling stupid for my mental freak-out, but I was still worried.

"He's a natural," the man said, retrieving the frisbee.

Opus sat on his hind legs, tongue hanging out the side of his mouth as he breathed hard.

"He never used to like to play fetch or with a Frisbee, but in the last year he's really come around to liking to play," Tina told them. "I have to run back inside now. I'll see you all later!"

"Bye, Miss," the second man said, as he walked past her, already getting his friend in a discussion about an upcoming baseball game.

"Oh, hey!" Tina said as she saw me. "Did you change your mind and want to jog?"

"No," I said, my voice a little shaky. "Come on inside. I want to show you something."

"Oh really?!" she asked, dropping me a wink. "Working on your story got your engine all fired up?" she teased, but she was walking with me, Opus now in lock-step, on Tina's left in the grass while I walked on the right, closer to the road.

"No, the person who was messing with my Mac sent me a message," I told her.

"Are they holding your files ransom? Did they get into your bank stuff? I know you were worried about—"

I'd pulled my phone out and showed her the picture. She looked at it, frowning, and almost walked into the door I'd pulled open so we could head into the lobby. Opus nudged her at the last second, and she looked where she was going and stepped into the safer area, within the jambs.

"This was from two summers ago," she told me handing the phone back, "Creepy message, but that's not from around here."

"But the mountains—"

"There's no snow on them. I was in Arizona near the Grand Canyon. They pulled this off of my Facebook," she said, pointing.

The screen was small, and I hadn't paid attention to the color of the stone, and now that she mentioned it, I felt like an ass. Still, it was creepy as hell. I tapped the picture of the band of money with the eyeballs.

"That's the same thing," I told her. "That was the song that was left on my Mac."

"I sort of remember that commercial. Since I've been doing a ton of social media for you, maybe somebody was being clever and letting you know they're following along?"

"Why would they have downloaded a picture of you to send to me though? I mean, it's not really a secret that we're a thing, though I haven't done much on Facebook until recently."

"Because I do, and I drop links whenever your book goes live," she said, as I hit the button to the elevator.

"You've been promoting my books?" I asked her, feeling even dumber now.

"Yeah, I've been coordinating with your VA. She thought it was kind of cute and said that because you're a man writing in a woman's genre, it might cut down on all the stalker-lady types from sending you unsolicited sext messages."

"Sext messages?" I asked, knowing what the term was, but not believing it because I knew my lady author friends got unasked-for penis pics from time to time.

I chalked that up to idiot guys giving our gender a bad name, not something that normally went on. Besides, the one nude pic somebody had sent me was of Pamela Anderson through messenger, and it was an old one from Playboy. *Did people really do that?* I guessed there was weirdness all over the internet and it made everyone much, much closer than they used to be in the world. Twenty-four-hour news cycles, Facebook, Facetime. It all made everything instantaneous.

I suddenly felt relieved.

"Yeah silly, where girls send you pictures of their... *you know*."

"Not really. I don't get those," I admitted.

"I know. I saw," she said, and stepped in the elevator as it opened.

I was surprised by that, but she had had my phone for

a good portion of two days. It only seemed natural she'd have looked at whatever popped up on the screen.

"Okay, it just... I got creeped out and worried somebody was out there on the street, taking pictures of you. It felt kind of threatening in the moment."

"I know," she said, and touched my arm. "But this time, I think it's just somebody trying to be cute."

"Okay," I muttered, and then stepped forward when the doors opened and walked toward our room.

Tina didn't say anything else until I got the door open. Opus bounded inside and barked happily, spinning in a circle and then sitting at attention near the snack bar.

"You didn't tell me you ordered me lunch!" Tina said rushing forward and sliding onto the stool next to my computer.

I didn't have the heart to tell her as I watched her dig in, even drinking the beer I'd started on for myself.

"Good thing I got some exercise in," she said around a mouthful.

I watched for another moment then walked over to the phone and dialed 1.

"Room service."

"Yeah, I need to order another burger, and a beer," I said and heard a whine behind me, "Better make that two burgers and a big basket of fries. Oh, let's add two more beers, this is going to be a long day."

"Hungry?" Tina asked, then took a long swallow of the beer and offered me the bottle.

"That's it," I said and hung up the phone. "Starving."

14

RICK

The day went by faster than I thought it would have. Opus and I got our food soon after the call, and I was deep into my editing. The sheer panic that had dumped buckets of adrenaline in my veins had washed away, and when I was done eating, editing and cleaning up my manuscript, I was tired. I fell asleep before 9pm, a record for me.

"I printed off the tickets," Tina said, waking me.

"Huh?" I asked her.

"Before we left Michigan. I got our tickets online and got the VIP pass to get in early," she told me.

I rolled over and was amazed that she had beat me awake. I was always the first one up in the mornings, by a long shot. I looked at the patio doors and saw it was black outside, I walked over to the doors and looked outside. We were high enough up that I could see the lights of the city.

"It's a beautiful view," Tina said, wrapping her arms around me.

I leaned back into her a little bit, feeling her warmth and put an arm around her.

"You bought and printed tickets out for the event before we left Michigan?" I asked her, finally feeling awake enough to finally understand.

"Yes, for all three days. Friday, Saturday and Sunday."

"Is the event dog-friendly?"

"Oh yeah, and I've already found out there's going to be a vendor there who does doggie vests. Opus can wear his own Kevlar and look tacktikool."

I laughed softly and turned to see the time on the small stove. Five a.m... it was early after all.

"Why are you up so early?" I asked her

"I'm kind of looking forward to going later on this afternoon."

That was... really kind of cool. She wasn't just pretending to be interested in something because I was. She was genuinely interested. Maybe I needed to quit thinking that she was only going to appease me and quit trying to find something for her to do that I thought she would think was interesting. In my goal of trying to keep her happy, I was working against her. The realization, I will admit, made me almost break out into an inappropriate grin. At least I'd realized it before it became an issue.

"I'm looking forward to having you and Opus come along," I told her truthfully. "There's going to be a lot of neat stuff to look at there."

"Did you know they have some RVs there?" she asked me quietly, her hands moving around to my back, kneading the spot in the middle of my shoulder blades that always seemed to hold my stress.

"Stan, the tire guy, and I talked about that," I said and heard Opus let out a groan as he stood and stretched.

"The tire guy? Oh yeah. The one who kept watching me run."

"I'm sure he was just a dog lover."

"Hey now," she said sharply, and the hands to the back were gone, replaced with a pinch to the side under my arm.

"*Owwwww*, I meant Opus," I said, realizing my slip of the tongue could be taken out of context.

The pinching fingers stopped and rubbed the hurt before I could say more. "Uh huh, I was just making an observation, and you implied I'm a dog—"

"No, I wasn't. I saw him checking you out, too. I was just deliberately not pointing that out."

"Because you're a big ball of maturity," she said, and came around the front to crack open the patio door.

Almost arctic-feeling air rushed in, and I felt Opus push his head between my knees as he studied the cool morning from behind the safety of a warm human. It was probably in the high thirties or low forties, but Tina stepped outside and walked to the edge of the balcony and took a deep breath. After a moment, I followed her, even though I had on only my sleeping pants. They might have featured a cartoon character, but I didn't care.

"Maybe I was a little bit immature," I admitted to her.

"Good. Now that's out of the way, let's get coffee going, go to breakfast somewhere and then go check out the town! Preppercon does its soft opening this afternoon, and there's a ton I want to see!"

"I've been asking for... Wait. What do you want to see?" I asked her.

"The Great Salt Lake," she said, without a moment's hesitation.

"Okay, let me go get the coffee going," I said and turned to head back to the kitchen. "You coming Opus?"

He chuffed, and I felt him brush against my leg in the darkened suite. After a moment, Tina came inside as I was finding the room's coffee pot and trying to decipher the directions to use it in the dark, with a caffeine-free brain. Always a recipe for disaster—

Tina turned on the light, and once I got my vision back, I finished the process. While it brewed, I grabbed my stuff and headed to the bathroom to get ready for the day.

Once I was showered and cleaned up, I headed out to the heady aroma of coffee. Tina was sitting next to my laptop I'd left up on the bar with two mugs. I sat down and looked into the one she slid over to me.

"It's empty," I said quietly, noting the pot was as well.

"Yeah, this was sooooo good, I had two cups. The only other coffee they put in the room is decaf."

Of all the evil things, stealing the last cup of coffee and leaving a caffeine junky with something that's been washed by formaldehyde or worse is cruel and unusual—

My mental whining was interrupted by a knock at the door. Tina slid off the stool, and I noticed she was wearing one of the big fluffy bathrobes that the hotel provided. I was about to ask her what was going on when she grabbed her small purse and opened the door. She pulled out some bills and said thanks and turned and walked back in, letting the door swing shut behind her. She set a large white insulated carafe down in front of me.

"They had your brand," she said, taking a sip and making a face. "The stuff you brewed is a little bit better than battery acid, but that's about it. This came from the restaurant downstairs."

"I love you," I said simply, and poured a cup.

Tina had been taking another sip of her coffee when I said that, and it spewed across the snack bar.

TINA WANTED TO SWIM IN THE GREAT SALT LAKE, BUT IT really wasn't warm, and she hadn't brought a suit. We could have bought one, but we walked the shoreline instead. Opus went into the water up to his knees, stuck his tongue out as if to take a drink and let the water run back out of his mouth immediately. He made sure to walk out slowly, so not to splash it all over.

"It looks like a regular lake," Tina said. "But I can smell the salt from here."

"Yeah, I did a little google research, and it looks like three rivers feed into here. The causeway sort of splits the northern sides up a bit, so the water looks different from the air. I guess it's something to do with what kind of algae can live at different salinity levels and stuff."

"You're such an adorable geek sometimes," she told me and leaned into my side.

I was about to hug her when Opus snarled at something that darted at the tree line, fierce barks erupting.

"Opus, *Nein!*" Tina called, and the dog came to a stuttering halt, his great paws making lines in the sandy area separating the beach from the shore we'd been walking down.

Opus's fur stood up, and he made a weird growling noise but didn't move. I got closer to him, and after a moment's hesitation, Tina did too. I put my hand on his scruff and realized he'd gotten quieter when I'd gotten closer, but his growl was that weird one he'd done before when he'd warned me at the house. I gave him a quick pet from scruff to tail and then in an almost unconscious act, patted my right side where I'd been carrying the Beretta.

"What is it, boy?" Tina asked, her voice shaking.

"He's making the same sound I told you about. I don't know what he's telling me," I told her.

Something crashed through the brush, and Opus almost took off running, but Tina caught his collar while he barked. His fur stood on end, and if it was possible for an already mutant looking hellhound to grow in size, he totally hulked out, saliva starting to run from the edges of his mouth.

"Opus, what is it? Bear?" Tina asked, looking at me.

"Does he know what a bear is?" I asked her.

"I don't think so. I've never seen him do this before," she told me.

"Let's get out of here," I told her.

"Right behind you," she whispered, and I noticed she had goosebumps running up and down her arms as she rubbed them.

"Opus, you keep an eye on your mom for me, buddy," I told him.

He barked a little louder than I expected but when I moved, he walked between Tina and the woods. We made it back to the van without incident, but almost bumped into somebody who was walking down the side-

128

walk. I stepped out of his way, and Opus bumped Tina over.

The man had his head down and was reading something on his phone intently by the look of things. Even still, I didn't have as much room to move as Tina did and I bumped shoulders with him.

"Sorry about that," he mumbled.

"Sorry," I mumbled in response, feeling better about what had happened.

Maybe Opus had seen a relative of the fuzzy-assed squirrels that he'd declared war on where we parked War Wagon. Maybe he was just angrily telling the squirrels out here in Utah that his ass was fuzzier and he would eat them for taunting him. Still, that weird growl had thrown me off. After hearing it again, it almost sounded like... fear?

"Want to get some food, or just go to the show?" I asked Tina.

"I want to go to the show," she admitted. "There's a booth I want to stop at."

"Oh? I didn't know you were going shopping?" I asked, feeling like a good teasing might cheer her up.

"It's a company that breeds and trains dogs like Opus."

I grinned. "Thinking about getting a puppy?"

"No, but they've got some cool stuff there, and one of these days, the trainer I bought Opus from is going to stop up there, and I wanted to say thanks to him."

I grinned, finally realizing her master plan. Well, I didn't realize it, she'd kept back that key piece of information and probably only let it slip now that she was a little bit unsettled. Hell, I'd joked with Opus that we'd have to get him a girlfriend someday, though I was jokingly telling him it was going to be a big Standard Poodle we'd name Fifi or something fancy in honor of his latest canine friend.

"What do you think, bud?" I asked Opus.

He barked.

"What did you ask him?" Tina asked me as I put my key in the lock of her door, opening it for her.

"If he wanted to go see the dogs and puppies at the show."

"I was standing right here. I didn't hear you say that."

I let Opus in the side door, and he was inside the van in a flash. I walked around and unlocked my side and got in as well. You can't reach the door locks unless you get out of the other seat and I always beat Tina to it anyway, so she'd quit trying to get it open for me.

Opus, of course, was already sitting in the middle of the seats, near the doghouse where the motor was still warm from the drive earlier.

"Well, it's all about body language and an innate understanding of canine communication."

Opus chuffed and Tina snorted a disgusted sound.

"No way, he didn't... no. You didn't ask, he just agrees with you to be a butthead to me."

Opus sneezed, which made Tina turn red in the face and made me laugh.

15

RICK

The show was fantastic. The first two days we walked around, talking to vendors. I couldn't help it. I had to check out the Apocalypse RVs that Stan and I had talked about. The one I loved was a converted Deuce and a half. It had all the modern conveniences that War Wagon had, but it was almost three feet higher off the ground. There was also a smaller version and a tricked out Humvee.

I found out the pricing for laughs and giggles, then reluctantly decided to stick with War Wagon instead of lusting for a half a million dollar BOV that would enable me and a team of ten to live out the zombie apocalypse in comfort, style and badassery.

Walking around, I also ran across something that caught my eye. There was a vendor there who was selling home sized freeze dryers. You could literally put any sort of food inside it, follow the instructions and process fresh or cooked produce and meals and turn it into something that could be stored for a long time. The unit itself was the size of a small washing machine. I grabbed a pamphlet, but realized that unless I was farming, gardening or buying huge bulk of fresh produce, it was something that was just a curiosity to me.

Tina and I spent some time talking with a husband and wife who were selling quick take-down geodesic dome framed tents. This especially caught my attention. The metal framework when taken down was heavy, but not as heavy as you'd expect it to be.

There were discussion panels, one with some of the authors I'd come to meet and get autographs from. The one I sat through, with a bored Opus and Tina, was about how to start prepping and how to use common items in unusual ways in a survival situation. Really, how to MacGyver some things. Then one of the authors was asked how to involve little kids in prepping.

His response was to introduce them slowly to it. Start off with Boy Scouts, camping. Work with the kids, hand in hand. Figure out what you need, make a list, pack and go do it. When you're all done, ask the kids if there was something they wanted but found out they didn't have. If they didn't have it, did they need it? Was it practical?

Then plan out a new trip. Make a new list. Keep pushing the envelope, maybe take a little less food, but plan on doing more hunting or fishing. There's no sense having a truly apocalyptic scenario and practice runs of getting on CBW gear if you're not getting them into the mindset of thinking for themselves in a potential survival situation - without calling it that.

I noticed Tina paid attention to that one a little bit, though I wasn't sure if it was the talk about getting the kids involved or the discussed increased parental involvement. I caught her look and grinned.

Busted.

She'd been thinking about kids.

Someday.

There was so much there, but the toy department was one area I wanted to visit, once I had my autographs from A. American and AR Shaw, the Watson's and Kate Morris. The toy department stocked everything a felonious-minded pen-monkey could ever dream of. Traps, knives, swords, guns. So many guns. Guns I'd only seen or heard of, including some stuff that Hickock45 from YouTube talked about.

The final day, I took my cash stash, something I had been forcing myself to go without until then. I had some serious itchy palms, and I knew some of the toys I wanted to buy weren't going to sell out. I was patient and made sure to talk to the vendors and learn as much as I could. Nobody could be an expert at everything, and the best thing I was good at (writing) I wasn't an expert on, so I weighed the pros and cons, and on the third day, I walked up to the firearms dealer while Tina was checking out the puppies for the eleventy billionth time.

I made her quit dragging me to the booth after the first nineteen times because I didn't need her to wear me down to get a puppy. I knew they were still too young for their forever homes, but when she wasn't looking, I'd already gotten a card from the trainer. Still, Tina didn't see the guy she'd got Opus from. I had asked her to let me know if she ran across him because I'd have liked to meet him, too.

"You sure you want the Kel-Tec?" the dealer asked, pulling a box out.

"Yeah, I remembered what you said and did some research. For my type of hiking and camping, I'm looking for something that will fit in my pack. If the Henry Survival Rifle wasn't in a .22, I kind of like that better."

"Yeah, .223/5.56 does have more kick to it. I hate to talk guys out of guns they want to buy though. Just know you won't be hitting quarters with a scope at a hundred yards. More like a two or three-inch grouping."

"I've got a heavier gun for my quarter eradication strategy," I grinned, thinking of my dad's rifle, handed down to me.

"No problem. What kind of magazines do you want? It comes with the basics but..."

"How about we mix and match some sizes. Two of each, whatever you have." I said, hoping I could get it all bagged, in the van and out of sight before Tina saw me.

This was a purchase made more out of want, than lust of something different and shiny that had no basis in need.

"Drum magazines too? You know it takes standard AR mags, right?"

"Yeah, I mean... How about one drum magazine?" I told him in response, and couldn't help but grin as he noticed that I was serious.

"Ammunition?"

"Not today," I told him, "I've already—"

"Rick!"

I turned to see Tina, with Opus at her side. On the other side of her was a familiar looking man with one hand on her shoulder, pointing at me.

"Craig?"

Piles of magazines and the box with the SU-16a were being heaped in front of me. "I'll be right back," I told the vendor.

"I'll start tallying this up for you."

"Thanks. A friend I haven't seen since high school just..."

"It's cool. If I get bored, I can help someone else," he told me, and I looked to see if he was being snippy, but he was smiling and made a head motion toward Tina and Craig.

I walked over with my hand out, smiling ear to ear.

"Craig, holy sh—"

"Wait, you know each other?!" Craig said, looking confused from me to Tina, and back again.

He had slimmed down a ton, and if I hadn't checked his message from the other day, I wouldn't have recognized him.

"Yeah. Tina, this is Craig, he's the old school buddy of mine who moved to Colorado!"

"Well, yeah, I know. Craig is the trainer who got me Opus," Tina said, suddenly acting awkward and strange.

"Holy shit, small world!" I told him.

"Yeah well... I didn't do all of it. I mostly train dogs for SAR work. When Tina contacted me looking for a protection dog, I got ahold of my breeder in Hungary who specializes in this kind of thing. Tina put down a deposit, and I flew out there and flew him home. He's good at what he does," Craig said, reaching down to pet him, but he backed up and pressed himself close to Tina, an action I'd seen him often do with guys around the female human he owned.

"That's crazy. How did you get into dog training?" I asked him.

"Well, I was originally a handler in the Air Force. When I got out a couple years ago, I started to breed pups, but most of my work is with training now."

"Did you bring any puppies with you?" Tina asked, looking at me slyly.

"No, I have somebody dog-sitting for me at my place for a few days so I could come up here. I can't believe you're out here, man. I haven't seen you in forever," Craig said, turning back to me.

I was excited to see him, but needed to finish my transaction. "Yeah, this is really cool. Hold on. I'll be right back. I'm checking out over here," I said, hooking a thumb over my shoulder.

Tina shot me a puzzled look, but I turned around and saw the vendor I'd been talking with smiling. He'd put the SU-16's box in a large shopping bag, and the magazines were stacked in two smaller woven bags.

"Wow, thanks. What's the damage?" I asked him.

He told me, and I tried not to choke, but I'd asked for two of every magazine and the total wasn't really that expensive. I looked over my shoulder at Tina who was talking to Craig again, Opus near her side, while I pulled out my money clip and then counted the bills. What a small world... I got my change and loaded up and walked back toward them.

"I'm heading outside to drop some stuff off, so I don't have to carry it around the rest of the day, do you guys want to come? Maybe grab some lunch and catch up?"

"I can't stay long," Craig said. "I've got some computer

work to do and a couple quotes to put together. I just drove up for the day though. Tomorrow is a workday."

"I can't believe you drove all this way to say hi," Tina said, smiling.

"It's no big deal. Not that far of a drive, as long as there's no ice on the highways. There was also a breeder friend I needed to get in touch with," Craig said. "But I can give you a hand out to your van."

I gave him a bag with magazines. He looked down and smiled when he saw what was in it.

"Stocking up?" he asked.

"Yeah, never know when you won't be able to get them anymore," I told him, smiling.

We headed out. "Hey, did you get a chance to go see A. American?" I asked him, nodding to the booth near the main aisle near the door.

"Author, right? Wrote the *Going Home Series*?"

"That's him—"

"I thought Rick was going to hump his leg. It was funny watching him meet one of his idols," Tina interrupted, grinning.

"That's a mental image I didn't need," Craig told her. "What do you think, Opus, you teach him that one?"

Opus was silent but made some sort of whining noise I took to mean a negative. Good boy, he was sticking up for me. Bros before yoyos. Craig stopped at the back of the van, and I juggled bags to my left hand so I could get to the keys. I opened the back and then slung my bags in, taking the bag from Craig as well.

"Wow man, you camping?" he asked, seeing the gear I had packed but hadn't yet used.

"We were talking about it, but we kept finding ourselves in hotels and motels," Tina spoke up.

"Ah, well, it sounds like fun. You guys should check out the Arches National Park if you're still planning on heading south."

"That's on my list," Tina said.

"Yeah, I had planned on it too, but it's good to hear we're on the same page. Hey, how's your little brother doing? I haven't seen him in a while.

Craig's face clouded over. "He died. It was about the time Tina here got Opus."

"Oh man, what happened? I'm sorry, I mean..." I stammered.

"No, it's fine, I know what you meant. It's just... my little brother got himself into a jam, and bad things happened. Still don't talk about it much."

"Sorry to hear that," Tina and I chorused at the same time.

If it weren't a somber moment, then I would have shouted "jinx!" and told Tina she owed me a coke. As it was, we both just let it go.

"Ancient history. I gotta run. Give me a shout if you're going to be headed my way!"

"I will," I said and shook his offered hand. "I'll see you around."

We said our goodbyes and I stood there with Tina and Opus watching him leave. The parking lot at the fairgrounds was huge, and he was soon lost in a minefield of vehicles.

"Wow, small world. You didn't tell me you knew Craig," I told her.

"I don't really. I answered an ad, put my deposit down

and got Opus. I went to somebody else for them to teach me the training commands my fuzzy buddy knew," she said, her words turning into a baby coo before recovering. "Craig was in the process of moving, but he had somebody local he'd recommended. I guess they work with the Genesee County Sheriff's Department."

"*Ahhh*, I see," I pulled her close and hugged her tight.

"What do you mean?" she asked.

"Nothing. Just weird that as small a world as this is... but man, it was good to see him. His little brother used to try to play with us as kids. Kind of a shock to hear that he's... dead."

"Yeah, he was kind of vague about that. Must have been bad. Drugs?"

"Could be," I admitted, "There was little else to do growing up in our town. It was mostly weed though."

"What about meth? Even at your place up north, meth was getting cooked up on the sly."

"I guess that's possible. Besides, we're gonna get married soon, so it's *our* place up north," I told her, closing the back door.

"So, what did you buy?" She asked me.

"A boomstick with a ton of magazines."

"Where's the ammo?" She leaned over and peered in the window.

I love this woman.

16

RICK

We left the day after I bought the SU-16 and saw Craig. Before that though, we'd gone back inside and bought a thousand rounds of 5.56 in different types, bullet weights, and different color tips. I knew some of those colors weren't necessarily legal in Michigan, but I didn't ask too many questions and paid cash for ammo. Unlike firearms, ammo didn't need a background check... yet. At least in Utah. I was thrilled that my California friends had had a couple bills shut down though. They were looking at a capacity limit on their magazines, and there were potential background checks for ammo purchases, I think.

I didn't pay too much attention to it, but since I'd been on the prepping forums more than the writer forums in recent months, I'd been more aware. Still, the civil unrest or loss of power due to a storm or man-made event was my biggest worry. That was what I mainly prepped for, but now that I'd been made more aware, I'd tried to learn more about things I knew I was weak on. Trapping for

140

one. I'd learned about trapping from my dad but I'd never really had an interest like he did in it. He made it look easy. Set a snare or trap, bait it, and come back and collect meat or something for fur.

So, I did what any modern-day person would do: I started watching YouTube videos. There was one channel called The Wild North, run by a wily Canadian named Andrew. It had gotten me some looks from Tina at the hotel while I'd watched his latest video about making a birch bark moose call, and the way he'd cuss up a storm raised her eyebrows, but it was entertaining, and I learned a ton of stuff about it. Heck, I'd even bought a snare kit on Amazon from a company my father used to order from directly.

"Where are we going to stop?" Tina asked me, breaking my inner monologue.

"I think it's up here a little bit," I told her.

"The scenery changed so much from Salt Lake City," Tina said. "It was like we were in the tallest parts of the mountains, and now it's turning into desert. Wait, don't say anything," Tina said, holding up her hand in a universal stop gesture.

Opus chuffed, and then put his nose in her side, rubbing his head against her ribs in a loving manner.

"I wasn't going to. Like you, I did a little googling myself and printed some maps out. Since you mentioned we were going to see the arches on my Facebook page, I got all kinds of tips on where to go, and I think it's time we should go do a little camping. Maybe a day or two?"

"I was hoping you were going to say that," Tina said, "I noticed that when you don't get to play in the woods for a while, you get... cranky."

"I'm an introvert, not a hermit," I told her. "I don't hate everyone, just—"

"Being around too many people. I know, I've gotten to know and grown to love your quirks. After being around people for three solid days, and I mean a lot of people... you're ready to soak up some solitude."

I really, *really* loved this woman.

"Yeah, I'm that predictable, huh?" I asked her.

"Yep. The question is, where are we going to camp?"

"I was hoping you'd ask that. What do you think about hiking in somewhere near the Double Arch? We'd have to park, hike in and find someplace, but there should be water, according to a topo map, in a canyon bottom we'd have to travel near."

"Just because it shows there's water there doesn't mean it doesn't dry up in the summertime," Tina said, pulling her phone out.

"Now you remember to charge it," I teased.

"Hey!"

Opus barked happily.

WE EXITED THE HIGHWAY AND TOOK THE ROADS AS indicated by my phone's GPS. It had lost signal a few times, but the route was pretty straightforward. We had a map, and road signs were pointing the way to the trailhead. We weren't alone either, there were a few cars behind us and RVs parked along the side of the road in what's called disbursed camping, or in the case of the RV, boon docking. The RVs had solar panels either hanging off the side, set up on the roof or on racks on the ground, weighted down with sandbags, probably filled on-site just for that purpose.

I marveled at that as I drove slowly. Opus had fallen asleep again, bored. He would have fun tonight, though. This was the desert, and the only thing more gorgeous than the scenery was my soon-to-be wife. It was a sappy thought, but this entire trip had been full of sappy thoughts. Probably my body's own defense mechanism to beat down the fear of meeting her father and mother. Yikes.

"There it is, there's our spot!" Tina said excitedly.

It wasn't a marked spot, nor the trailhead, but instead, she'd been looking for a place for us to pull off, set up the groundsheet, the tent... but this was right next to the road.

"You want to park so close to everyone else?" I asked her, confused.

"No silly. Park here, but look up there," she said pointing.

If I hadn't been going so slow, I might have veered off the road. Instead, I looked at the spot she was pointing to off to my left. It was part of the... hill, mountain... but it had flattened out, and there were some drifts of sand mixed in the rocky area.

"It might be a little chilly up there without much of a windbreak," I told her. "I don't think we can have an open fire."

"You and Opus will keep me warm," she shot back immediately.

She had a point.

I grinned.

I'd packed the cold sleeping bags I'd kept in the

motorhome, knowing the nighttime temperatures dropped. When she said Opus and I would keep her warm, that meant she usually sprawled atop of me with Opus curled up in whatever space was left... if we let him. I wasn't about to let him sleep outside, so I guessed I'd have to rough it. I grinned again.

"Ok, but if it gets too cold, we'll come back to the van and warm up, or sleep in here."

"Aye-aye, Captain," she said, throwing me a jaunty salute.

Opus, of course, barked happily, having woken up in the middle of the conversation to put his two cents in. I pulled off where instructed and realized it was actually a perfect spot. The ground was relatively flat, and I wouldn't be in the way of traffic and, more importantly, my van wouldn't get stuck.

That was something I'd learned when I'd first got it. Parking on a soft shoulder with a big vehicle... it's not pleasant. I shut the motor off, and as soon as I cracked my door, Opus jumped over my seat and was out in a flash.

I was about to say something but Tina's look stopped me, and she nodded toward Opus, who was squatting at a bush, before walking around to every single bush that had the audacity to push its way through the rocky and sandy soil, to mark his territory. It was also obvious I should have stopped for him to go to the bathroom sooner. I made a mental note of that for next time and stretched.

We'd been on the road for a while, and nighttime was about to catch up to us. I heard Tina get out and then she went around to the back of the van and opened the double doors.

"So, you going to teach me how to shoot this?" She pulled out the box of the SU-16 I had somewhat shame-facedly hid from her.

"I've never shot one myself. I don't know if we're allowed to shoot here. I'll have to look it up," I admitted, though I was kind of interested in seeing what the lead spitter was capable of.

"There's nobody around us. There was further back there, but it's getting late now and all the day-trippers have left."

"That's true."

"Plus, if you don't want to weigh it down in your pack, I'll carry it. You've still got your pistol."

I opened my mouth and then closed it before I got myself into trouble. As girly as Tina was around me, I often forgot she had a tomboy streak a mile wide. It reminded me of her wanting to play laser tag and paint-ball and her girl's league of roller derby that was taking a break for the season and... she was everything I was *and* wasn't. So instead of sticking my foot into it, waxing sappy, I went with it.

"If you want to, I'd love to figure out how to shoot it together, *with* you."

"See. You're a fast learner," she said, tearing open the packaging.

I grinned and got my basic bug-out bag out of the back and then reached back further for my bigger back-packing pack. Tina didn't stop unboxing the Kel Tec, but she watched as I snapped my day-pack-sized B.O.B. to the larger pack that already had a sleeping mat rolled and tied onto the bottom. I had an integrated camelback, basi-cally a chamber for water with a straw for the person to sip on, but it was empty. I worked on filling that without making a mess, and by the time I was done, Tina had the gun unpackaged, had figured it out and was dry fitting the two small magazines that came with it.

"What do you call this?" she asked.

"A gun? It's a Kel-Tec SU-16C I think. I don't think it's the B."

"No, the black gun *look*. Tackticool? I'll have to remember to get Opus's vest out and put it on him so he can get in on the fun with us. I bet your fans would love to see all of us—"

Tina's phone rang, interrupting her train of thought and she put the gun down and pulled it out of her pocket.

"Missed call. It was Craig, wait..."

Her phone let out a chirp, a notification for a voice-mail or text message. She did some swiping as I put everything together for my loadout and then pulled out the pack she'd made to carry in her truck. We'd have to add a little bit of clothing, her sleeping bag to go with mine, the small two-person backpacking tent was already in my supplies... and then we could argue over food and who was going to cook and how much water we wanted to lug up to her spot and—

Tina looked up at me. "Craig called, must have bad reception up here because it only rang once."

"Did he leave a message?"

"Yeah, said he got a call from that trainer in Germany he got Opus from. They had a canceled order for an intact girl. Since the person who canceled paid a deposit and won't get it back, they were trying to sell the dog and were coming up dry, so they were reaching out to others in the states to see if anybody needed one. She's like eighteen months old, kind of young for old boy Opus here, but…"

"When we get good reception…" I paused as Opus came up and sat down at attention in front of me, his big brown eyes boring holes in me. "How about you tell him we're interested?"

"I don't know how much she's going to cost!" Tina was red in the face, and her hands were shaking.

"You don't want a poodle for a lady friend, do you?" I asked Opus.

He looked at me for a long moment, then over at Tina who'd bit her lip, then back at me. He sneezed.

"So, you want a young lady to work with? Maybe see if there's some romance involved someday? She'd be just like you, a fantastic specimen of what you are, Furface."

Opus chuffed, but he was so quiet I almost lost his response when a soft moan of wind came over the rocks. I didn't think Tina even heard it, because she was looking at me in either surprise or horror.

I bent down to his level. He barely moved.

"I couldn't hear you. Do you want us to see if we can find you a girlfriend? Maybe somebody to raise a litter of pups with?"

Again, he chuffed, real quiet.

"I can't hear you, buddy."

He barked, and Tina about fell over. I stood back up, petting him between the ears, my hand kneading the spot in the back of his left ear like he loved.

"So, yeah. Let's do it. I've kind of wanted to but didn't want to push, and I got the idea you wanted to, and now we know Opus does want to."

She hesitated. "But…"

"Call it an early or belated wedding present," I told her.

What happened next would almost be described as X-rated and even Opus crawled under the van for a moment until Tina and I finally broke apart. Good thing there was nobody in sight of us. That was when I noticed the sun was setting, and if we were going to get set up in the daylight, we'd have to get a move on. I put on my pack, strapping it across my chest and waist. Tina put the gun in her bag with a magazine, and a box of .223. Then she got her sleeping bag and handed me the larger soft-sided cooler. She filled her hands with two single-gallon jugs of water and wordlessly we started up the hillside.

Setting up camp doesn't have to be difficult, but sometimes I found myself making it more work than it actually needed to be. I found a spot in the sandy hillside that didn't have large rocks and then rolled out the ground-sheet. Opus walked across it as I was getting it in place and he chuffed as if to give me approval for an unasked question.

"Dude, move," I told him as I rolled out the tent.

"He wants something," Tina told me.

"What do you want, buddy?" I asked him, pausing what I was doing.

He turned his head sideways and then walked around in a circle and laid down.

"You can't sleep there, I have to get the tent up. Don't you want to go see if there are any rabbits in the area around here to chase?" I asked hopefully.

He yawned and put his head down between his paws.

"I don't think you impressed him with your pathetic

attempt," Tina said, and I could tell she was about to laugh.

"Come on boy," I said shaking the tent out and standing at the edge of the groundsheet.

Opus opened one eye at me and then closed it again. I had a thought. I fluttered the tent out like I was going to set it up right over the dog, but when the nylon fabric covered him, the dog let out a soft snore. I could understand being tired, but this mutt had been sleeping on and off for most of the drive today. There was no way he was tired, even if he was only sleeping out of boredom.

"Dude..." I pleaded, pulling the tent off and letting it settle near Tina's feet.

Opus opened one eye again. Frustrated, I reached for his collar, and he lunged. I pulled my arm back at the last second, and his teeth got nothing. Then the fuzzy terrorist barked once and rolled on his back, wiggling his back and butt against the groundsheet before getting to his feet, his back legs tensing.

"I think he wants to play rough," Tina said quietly.

I'd played rough with him plenty of times, and although he'd startled me for a second there, I knew he wouldn't have gotten me... but he'd sent a very clear message.

Ham.

He was practically an Easter ham the way he'd been hamming it up in his acting and I looked around, spotting a rare piece of wood that had come to rest under a bush, a branch that had snapped off and been washed down till it caught under one of the shrubby bushy plants we were planning on using for a windbreak. Opus's eyes went where mine were and we both dove.

Well, I dove. He lunged.

I might have gotten it half a heartbeat before he did, but I was trying to get the stick and avoid crushing him. He knew I outweighed him, and had no problems using his shoulder and mass to try to get there first. I laughed as he pulled back, a playful and full-throated growl coming out of his jaws.

"I'll work on this, you boys have fun," Tina called from behind me.

I pulled harder, but I was trying to be careful not to pull too hard and break teeth. I was slowly pulling him to me, his feet scrabbling in the mix of sand and rock. I was about to declare victory when he changed tactics and pushed forward. I wasn't expecting that, and off balance, he pushed the stick into my stomach. I tumbled back-ward with the slope. When I got up, Tina was laughing, and Opus was sitting about eight feet away, the stick between his front paws as he laid in front of it.

"That's how it's gonna be?" I asked.

He barked happily. I darted forward, and he waited for the last instant, until I almost had my hands on it, to make his move.

"I'll get dinner going, too," Tina said.

But as we started another game of tug of war, I wondered how she was going to manage all of that while laughing her fool head off.

17

TINA

Tonight, she'd get the shotgun out from under the bed and load it and pray she wouldn't need it. Next, she'd Google dog breeders. She wanted something big, mean, and loyal. She had happened to stumble across a Facebook ad about a local breeder of German Shepherds. She'd have to do the training with the puppy, but—

The sound came from the bedroom, and the thump was felt through the wall she'd placed one hand on to brace herself while she looked at her reflection in the mirror. Thump. Something sounded like it scraped across the closet door on the wall on the other side of the mirror.

Dread filling her, she opened up the bathroom door, ready to bolt. Instead she saw the empty hallway in the house where she'd grown up with her parents. The door to her old bedroom was closed tight, as it had been since she'd bought the mini-storage from her mom and dad. Her bedroom (her parents' old one), had its door slightly ajar.

Had she closed it? She thought she had, but there was an inch of it open, and the murmur of soft music wafted out. She knew she hadn't turned on the radio, and the soft glow of the bedside lamp illuminated the sliver of open space between the door and the jamb. She knew she should pull her phone out and call 911, she knew she should go to her car, lock herself in, but this was a replay and she couldn't stop what she knew was coming next.

She watched as her hand pushed the door open, the hinges squeaking as the door swung in toward the left wall. Rose petals were spread from the doorway to the bed, which looked crimson as it had been covered. Sprawled out on top of her comforter, naked as the day he was born, was Lance. That was enough to make her heart almost stutter to a complete stop, but what was worse was what he had in his hand.

She'd later find out the knife was a Ka-Bar, and he was rubbing the blade along his chest, small scratches from the razor edge noticeable, blood dripping down his body and onto the petals below.

"It's about time you quit ignoring me, bitch."

"Lance, you can't be here," Tina stuttered, reaching for her phone in her pocket.

"Put it on the floor," Lance commanded.

So many times, he'd used his fists and words to beat her into submission that she almost complied, but she had been a strong woman before him and she'd found the core of steel in her soul once again, that for a short time, she'd lost.

"Get out now," she said in a voice that sounded confident, but she remembered she'd been trembling and scared and her courage had surprised her almost as much as it had Lance.

He blinked and shook his head as if realizing she'd said something he couldn't believe he was hearing.

"I said—"

"Get out now, or I'll call the cops," Tina repeated and was

about to hit the send button when Lance made a sudden movement.

Tina jerked her head as the knife flashed past, sinking into the wood of the door. She turned to run and hit the button at the same time and clipped the doorway instead. She stumbled and was tackled from behind. She was thrown to the ground under the weight of her ex-boyfriend, him easily towering over her.

In her dream, she remembered her rough and tumble days as a tomboy, and how she had a friend who was obsessive about Aikido and how they used to play and practice as young pre-teens. She went with the movement, and used his momentum as she rolled on her back and pistoned with her legs and threw him clear. Never before had she had this work out the right way, but instead of patting herself on the back she prepared to flee, she realized that she'd thrown him between the exit and herself.

Lance struggled to his feet as she made her choice. She ran to the bathroom, slamming the door behind her. She shot the lock and was working the small eye bolt lock her father had put in when she was little when the door shuddered.

"You bitch, come out HERE!" Lance screamed.

Tina backed up and hit the call button.

"Get away from me!" she shrieked.

"911, what's your emergency?" a voice said, but was so quiet she could hardly hear.

"I'm in the..."

Lance shrieked and bang on the door so hard that it deafened her.

In a blind panic she pulled out drawers. A weapon, she needed a weapon. Her right hand was full, so she tossed her phone as another blow hit the door, the jamb starting to break, the sound like an ice cube with warm liquid pouring over it, cracking. She pulled open her makeup drawer.

There!

"Please state your emergency," she heard as the door shattered, blowing open, the darkness, her fears now manifested in Lance.

His fists were bloodied, drool ran down one side of his mouth and his forehead was bruised and bleeding. Had he used his head? His knuckles were in worse shape.

"I've got something for you," he said, one hand going to his crotch.

"Oh yeah?" Tina said, her voice coming out, high pitched, the panic almost ready to take control.

"You're going to love it, and afterward, we're going on a trip. Of all the girls who've gone there, you'll be the only one who's gone while alive."

Tina had always prided herself on being strong-willed, unflappable and thought she could always do whatever it was a man could do. What she realized in that moment, was that at some point, Lance had broken her. Her body broke, and she knew that this time he was going to kill her.

"You had to have known it was going to come to this," Lance said, reaching for her.

"Lance... don't," she said softly.

"If you want, I can make it quick. You know... after we're finished in the bedroom..."

"I don't want to remember it," Tina said softly.

"I'll make it quick, then. I loved you once—"

He'd stepped in close, and the scissors she'd been hiding behind her back came out in a flash, four inches of gold colored steel piercing his side. He stopped abruptly as both hands slapped over his left side, one hand pulling the scissors out slowly. Blood spurted. Tina almost gagged but was moving again, her training with Adam coming back to mind. Eyes, balls, throat and kidneys. She faked a punch at his throat and when his hands came up, her knee went crashing into his unclothed and unprotected testicles.

He fell over sideways, his entire body spasming in pain, blood gushing from the spot where she'd stabbed him. Tina bolted, grabbing the phone as she ran, praying.

"Ma'am, are you there?" She heard as she ran down the hallway and into the kitchen of the mini-storage.

"Bitch!" Lance screamed over her shoulder.

"Please help me," Tina said in a calm voice over the phone, working the door handle lock and the deadbolt.

"I've already traced the call, troopers are on the way. Are you safe?"

"Bitch!" Lance screamed, stumbling to his feet in the hall-way, "I'll fucking kill you."

"Please hurry," Tina said and ran out the door and into the main office where she'd grabbed the master set of keys to the storage units.

"Ma'am, you need to go to a safe space—"

"Bitch!!!!!!!"

RICK

I woke up in the middle of the night to hear something howling in the distance. I had to pee because, when it had gotten cool, Tina had used my bladder to curl up on and Opus was laying on my feet. I had found out on our first unofficial date that she was a heavy sleeper. A few beers had relaxed her enough back then to make her zonk, and as long as I took it easy now, I wouldn't wake her. I found the edge of the zipper and opened it slowly, feeling like I was a balloon that was about to burst.

I felt Opus stir as I slowly extricated myself from the sleeping bag and crawled to the front of the tent and unzipped the door.

"I have to pee," I told Opus. "You want to go outside?" I asked, hoping that he did so I wouldn't get a cold nose to the ear in another couple hours, waking me again so he could leave his mark all over.

He got up and stretched and followed me out. The desert air was cooler than it had been in the evening, I'd been expecting it, but it was worse than I thought it would be. Opus ran off immediately and began marking bushes all around the campsite. I stretched, again. I found a likely spot, and while I was standing there, I heard Opus let out a strange warning growl. I'd heard that growl on two different occasions now, and both times had not understood what it meant. I couldn't see him in the dark, but I knew he was really close. I walked toward the sound of his growl.

He'd come to a stop between two bushes looking downhill in the general direction of where I'd parked the big van. His growl seemed to soften and went down in volume when I put my hand on the back of his fur. He looked up at me for a second and then cut the growl off completely.

"What is it, boy?" I whispered softly.

Opus looked out into the night. I had to wonder how much better his sight was than mine. Out there in the darkness, everything was vague, and at some point, clouds had rolled in covering any moonlight that might've lit the area around me. I could barely make out anything more than 10 feet away, but I knew Opus had either heard, smelled, or saw something that had put him on edge.

"Let's go, buddy," I told him, patting him on the flank and turned to go toward the tent. I got about eight steps before I realized he wasn't coming with me, I turned, and I could see that he was still standing in the same spot, but he'd sat down as if to stand guard.

"Opus," I hissed quietly. "If there's something out there, we gotta go tell your mom."

Opus turned his head and looked back at me, then reluctantly got up and headed on silent feet to me. We both walked back to the tent, and my night vision was destroyed when a flashlight turned on.

"What are you two doing?" Tina asked, with the flap of the tent open.

She was sitting up with the sleeping bag wrapped around her body twice, trembling and shaking.

"We went out to go use the bathroom, but Opus is warning me about something. He's doing that strange growl again."

"We don't know what that is. He's probably just being a goofball."

"He might be being a goofball, but I don't think he's ever told us wrong," I whispered softly, standing just outside the tent.

"Opus, what is it, boy?" Tina asked him. Opus stuck his nose inside the tent, where Tina pet his face. He made the odd growling sound again and then backed up and turned around, facing downslope.

"What's got you up so early?" I asked Tina.

"You weren't here, and it's cold outside. I lost my heating pad. And then my feet got cold because the little furry traitor would rather be with you."

That sounded a little bit like sore at me, and it wasn't something I wanted to get into while I was only half awake. Still, what Opus had alerted on was still a puzzle to me, and he was still tense. We could both see it in the way he was holding himself, and he was vocalizing that there was something going on.

I knew that, over the past year or so, I'd come to understand the dog's body language and his vocalizations. If I had kids, it was how I would imagine how a parent learns what their toddlers are saying through their gibberish before they learn to speak proper English. I could usually tell with a head tilt, a chuff or even his body language what he was trying to say, or the general idea of what he was thinking. I had read once that German Shepherds were capable of understanding over two hundred commands. That was just two hundred actions they're supposed to be memorizing. What happens though, is that I think dogs like him also understand normal speech. As a writer, I'm used to feeling like I'm a little bit crazy sometimes, but on this, I was fairly certain that I wasn't. Something was wrong, and I needed to find out and make sure we were all safe.

"Tina, would you slide me my holster," I asked her softly.

Tina turned and reached into the front of my day pack and unzipped it and then handed me my Beretta still in the holster. I couldn't make her features out, but as soon as I tucked the holster to the side of my pajama pants, she shrugged the blanket off and crawled out, grabbing both her shoes and mine.

"Put these on," she said quietly.

When I'd taken my shoes off earlier, I'd rolled the socks up in each shoe so I wouldn't lose track of them. When I'd gone out, I did what any Michigan boy would have done. I'd gone out barefoot, and from not wearing shoes for a large chunk of the season, my feet were tough like well... old shoe leather. It was mostly sand here, but there were rocks. If I hadn't been such an idiot before, I sure felt like one now. How many different types of snake, scorpion, spiders or any other creepy crawly creatures could I have stepped on in the dark? Unlike Michigan, where there's only a couple of venomous creatures, my

Google research had told me that the further south we went the more venomous things were.

I brushed sand off of my feet and put on my socks one foot at a time while trying not to fall over. When I got those on, I stood up straight because I realized in the middle of all of that, Opus had walked away from Tina and me. I could only see about six to eight feet away now that the flashlight was off, and he wasn't within the cone of my sight.

"Where did he go?" I asked Tina softly.

Tina whispered, "He went in the direction you two had come from."

I moved slowly, watching the ground and following my own footsteps. It didn't take very long for me to find where Furface had gone to. He was sitting in the same spot he had been before, and Tina and I moved up to him slowly. Tina was looking left and right, but I was trying to look in the direction that Opus was staring. All I saw was darkness.

"Let's move toward the van," Tina whispered.

I nodded. That was my thought as well. Tina whispered a command to Opus and, when I moved past him toward the van, he stayed right at my side with Tina behind us. We'd talked about this once, in a situation where there might be something dangerous happening. It wasn't that she was a girl, and it wasn't that she was almost a hundred pounds lighter than me, and it also wasn't because she didn't have a gun. She did, but just not on her. She did this because she knew that no matter what happened Opus and I would get in the way first.

Besides, of everyone here, Opus was the one with the best training. He'd be our first line of defense if something happened. We made our way as quietly as we could, and Opus hadn't repeated the low growl that he'd been using.

A big shape loomed near the roadway, and for a second my heart stopped.

When I realized it was the van, my heart stopped stuttering and started to work properly again. I let out a deep breath and motioned Tina to come forward.

"I can't see anything," I told her. "How's your night vision?"

"I can't see anything in the van. Your tinting is too dark in the back windows." She turned and gave Opus a command I hadn't heard before.

It was two short words, that sounded low and guttural coming out of her mouth. Opus seemed to stand at attention, and then his nose went to the ground, and he worked in a semi-circle around the van. I kept my hand close to my side where the gun was holstered and followed along as softly as I could. Opus began at the driver's side door and then walked around the back toward the rear end. He'd first smell the ground, and then he'd lift his head and sniff near the doors before taking another step in moving around again.

When he got around to the passenger side, he lifted a leg near the rear wheel after he sniffed it, and sprayed it with a trickle of urine. That had me wondering, and when he got to the passenger door where Tina always rode, he lifted his head and sniffed the air again. He let out a weird low growl, the one I'd heard before.

"What does is it mean?" I asked no one in particular.

"I don't know," she whispered. "I've only heard that

one other time, at the Great Salt Lake. I think it meant he was nervous."

Somewhere in the darkness further away than either of us could see, we both turned as we heard a car door shut. Opus ran back around to the side of the van and stood in front of Tina. As quietly as I could, I walked to him.

"Do you remember anyone parking near us?" I asked Tina.

"No. I picked a spot because there was no one around and I saw the spot where we could get some sleep without disturbing anyone."

I thought about that and decided I felt naked with only one gun and no spare magazines.

"Hold on, I'm going to get something. Don't look at the light. It'll kill your night vision. Opus, watch my back." I told them.

I hadn't locked my van, something I should have done. I had my preps in there, but there was no one out here, and after I'd gotten that kiss from Tina, I hadn't thought about it. At least I wouldn't have to go back up the slope in the dark to find my keys, so I walked around of the driver's side door and opened it up. I reached under the seat and pulled out the small fire-safe that I used to lock my gun in when I went into a store or place that had a no-gun policy. I thumbed in the code and slid the case open slowly. I grabbed the two spare magazines and closed it and slid it back under the driver's seat.

"I thought you said the light was going to come on?" Tina asked me softly.

That was when it hit me. The dome light had never come on. That was strange, strange enough for me to pull the Beretta out of the holster and take a step into the driver's side of the old Dodge.

The dark was absolute, unlike what little light had filtered outside. It was dark outside, but it was more about the lack of anything light on the inside that made it so dark. When I'd first gotten the van, all of the windows had been heavily tinted with the exception of the front and the two side windows. Everything from the driver's section back was limo-black. That made it great for camping, but it really sucked when suddenly your guard dog is nervous, and things aren't working right.

I couldn't see anything, and I tried to remember if I'd left a flashlight anywhere. My van didn't have one of those variable switches where I could turn the light off and on. If the door was open, the light simply came on. Very old-school, but very effective. That was when I got the thought. I reached for the knob and pulled it back, expecting my headlights to come on. The wash of light that would come through the un-tinted front window would be enough for me to make sure nothing was sneaking up on me in the dark of the van. It was a silly thought to feel that paranoid, but that's exactly what I did.

When, to my shock, the headlights didn't come on, a bead of sweat rolled down the back of my neck and down between my shoulder blades. It felt like an ice cube making a slow journey, and I couldn't help but shiver.

I pressed the horn on the steering wheel. *Nothing.* I pressed on both sides, activating both horn switches. *Nothing.* I scrambled out of the van and remembered to hit the light switch before I closed the door.

Adrenaline started dumping, my breath came out in small gasps.

"Rick!" Tina whispered loudly. "Calm down. What's going on?"

"Something's wrong with the battery in the van. It won't... hell, the lights aren't working, the horn isn't working, and the dome light's out. Something happened to the battery and we're too far away from civilization."

"Let's just go back to the tent, if anything comes around Opus will let us know," Tina said tensely.

"If I have to fix, this I'd rather do it while it's cool."

Opus chuffed, but very quietly.

19

RICK

I popped the latch on the hood and winced at the loud sound. I was going for quiet because I had a really bad feeling. I knew that the feeling had probably very little to do with reality, but all of this had been making me a little bit paranoid.

The other times I'd had a freakout moment it hadn't turned into anything. Still, it felt like somebody had been messing with me, and whether or not I liked it, I felt like I was playing *their* game with *their* rules. To what end, I didn't know. I was about to pull my cell phone out of my pocket to use it as a flashlight when I realized it was still back at the tent.

"What do you need?" Tina whispered at my side, both arms wrapped around herself as she shivered.

"I can't find my phone, I need the light—"

She interrupted me by pulling out the flashlight she'd been using earlier. I mentally cursed myself for getting all worked up in the dark of the van. I'd forgotten she'd had that. Of course she had it; she was better prepared than I was. All I could think was 'get a gun' and check on my soon-to-be wife. Understandable, but what am I going to shoot at in the dark when I can't see?

"Thanks," I told her and then for laughs and giggles turned the flashlight on quickly, checking the van out.

It was empty.

There was nothing and nobody lurking, waiting to eat the top of my head off. Nothing hideous with long arching claws to shred and render flesh. Even feeling foolish, this put me at ease. Light, something so simple and fundamental. It took away the uncertainty, the unknown.

Feeling relieved, I got out and shut the door and finished putting the hood up with the assistance of the light. Right away I could see the problem.

The battery was *gone*. The wires were disconnected and dangled uselessly.

"Omigod. We need to go," Tina hissed, having seen it too. "Let's take our phones and walk somewhere we have reception to call for help."

Her voice turned into a quiver at the end, and I understood the feeling entirely. Somebody had done this. You don't accidentally lose a battery.

"Opus, with me," Tina said in a more forceful tone.

I clicked off the flashlight and waited half a second. Tina put her hand in mine, and I walked back the direction the tent was in. I didn't want to use the light to make things easier. I think I'd used it too much already. In the distance, a howl went up, and Opus stopped, stiff-legged. He barked loud and aggressively.

"Opus, *nein*," Tina said and let go of my hand to grab his collar.

He'd already moved toward her, so she didn't have to latch onto him.

For a second, I had wondered if he was going to run after something. We began moving again, slowly. I had no idea what time it was, but surely it must be close to morning. We went agonizingly slowly, trying to not make a sound. Since Tina had told Opus to knock off the barking, we'd not said a word. Instinctively, we all knew we weren't alone out here and we were trying not to make any sort of sound. *Were we being hunted?* My mind was pregnant with ideas, and none of them were good.

"I know you're out here," a male voice shouted as the wind picked up.

We jerked to a stop.

"Who's that?" I stupidly asked Tina in a whisper.

Opus growled quietly.

"I don't know," Tina hissed back.

Gunshots rang out, barking loudly in the quiet night.

The dirt kicked up to our right. I pulled Tina to the ground as what sounded like an entire magazine was emptied in our direction. None of the shots really came close, so the person doing the shooting was firing at noises. We held our breath and tried not to move.

How Opus kept silent at that moment was a mystery to me. I wanted to yell back. I'd drawn my gun, but without being able to see the muzzle flashes, I didn't know where the shots were coming from, other than near our van.

Tina broke away from me and crawled toward the tent with Opus still at her side, belly crawling as well. Another dog let out an excited bark, but it wasn't ours. It was somewhere downhill.

"I'll make it quick if you come out. Make me track you, I'll kill you both slowly." The voice was full of rage, the words nearly unrecognizable.

"Got the packs," Tina said, pushing my big one to me.

"Get yours on, but stay low. He's shooting at sound, and I think he's got a dog tracking us."

I didn't have much time, but I didn't want to run through the darkness with my large bag. Almost everything I needed was in my smaller pack, including two quart-sized jugs of water. I unclipped my daypack and was shrugging mine on when Opus growled. I turned to see him focused behind us. Out of time, I put mine on as well, trying to get a fix on whoever was shooting.

"Last chance," the voice screamed. "Ten, nine, eight..."

"Hurry!" Tina said. I was all too glad to follow her as she moved out at a brisk pace.

LEAVING THE VAN, THE TENT AND ALMOST EVERYTHING behind, we hurried away, alternating between walking and jogging. There was no time for talk... only time to get away. We'd stop and talk when we felt safer.

In the last year, year and a half, I'd been reaching levels of fitness I hadn't been in since I was a kid. The jogging at the gym or with Tina and Opus had done a lot for my endurance, and I'd started lifting, though not heavily as I wasn't trying to bulk up. I had just wanted to turn myself into an efficient writer in good health. One thing most full-time writers seem to suffer is poor health, because of lack of exercise. I'd changed things, but what it hadn't prepared me for was doing this while terrified, and having a pack on my back.

At first, it was difficult to see, but Tina had taken the lead. When Opus went ahead of her a few steps, I followed behind them closely. I didn't know if he knew where we were going because I didn't, but he led us around and past large rock outcroppings that might have tripped us if we had been running full tilt. He was starting to pant, and I had been for some time now.

"Hold on," I said, finally coming to a stop after a few stuttering steps.

Opus came back to me, tongue hanging out, and pushed his head against my hip. An Opus hug. I shrugged out of my pack and dropped it on the ground. It was getting light out now, so it had to have been close to early morning. Daybreak wouldn't be that far behind. I dug into my pack and pulled out the green plastic quart canteen I kept in there. I'd refilled it in Salt Lake City. Tina saw what I was doing and did the same, looking behind me at the direction we'd fled from.

I drank deeply, but cut it off far sooner than I really wanted to. I wanted to avoid cramping or throwing it back up.

I cupped my hand and poured it in slowly. "Opus," I said, and he came forward and lapped it out of my hand, not paying attention to the splashes of water that hit his face as I kept pouring.

I had a tin pot I could have used but it was packed deep, and this worked fine. The dog had kissed me on the lips, so having his tongue on my fingers didn't faze me.

"We didn't leave too many tracks," Tina said. "At least, from what I can see."

"Good. Did you recognize the voice?"

"No. You?"

"No." Suddenly, I remembered. The phones! "Did you get our phones?" I asked her, seeing that she was still in her sleeping outfit she wore when we camped—a pair of sweats.

"No," she said softly. "I wasn't getting reception out here, so I left my phone in my jeans when I went to bed."

"Me too," I admitted, and sighed. It wasn't either of our faults. Thinking about holes in our guts had won out over remembering the phones.

"Are we safe to stop for a little while?" she asked, her eyes pleading.

"I think so," I said. "I haven't heard anything, but I think whoever it is has a dog."

"I heard it too," she said softly, finishing off a water bottle she had pulled from the top of her pack.

She sat down next to me. A little bit of dust puffed up and I noticed that where we were now being rockier than the red stone and sand that had been near our camp. I didn't say anything as Tina pulled her pack closer and got out the SU-16. I remembered she'd shoved it in there, and I knew it was in the tent, but in the heat of the moment, I hadn't thought to get it out. She quickly snapped it together and then pulled out one of the two magazines that came with it from the stock, and then a box of shells and loaded it.

I watched in silence. Who was chasing us? Was it the person who'd been sending me creepy messages? I knew I was freaked out, but Tina, the woman who'd bought a guard/attack dog, was the one who seemed like she was completely in control as she expertly put the gun together, loaded it, put it on safe and sat it across both of our backpacks.

"What do you think? Crazy fan?"

"I don't know. God, I hope not," I said, fearing it was.

Had I done something online that had pissed somebody off? Was there a lonely housewife out there with a jealous husband? Was this something altogether different?

"It sounded like a man. Deep voice. The dog... I think that's what woke me up. I heard something howl. Then I think we heard it twice more."

"I couldn't tell what kind of dog it was by the sound," Tina said.

"Sorry, I'm babbling. I counted off twenty rounds fired at us. That kind of has me off my game," I admitted, hardly handling my fear, amazed that Tina was holding up so strong.

"You know how to handle guns, the same way I do," Tina said, picking up the SU and offering it to me.

I shook my head no, feeling my breathing slow as my heart rate got back to normal.

"Do you think he's coming after us?" Tina asked.

"It'd be stupid to disable our van and try to shoot us if he was going to turn around and leave, wouldn't it?"

"I wonder if it was that drunk from the bar?"

Oh shit. I hadn't thought of that, but we'd run into him late into our trip, and the shenanigans had started when we'd gotten back from up north after saying our goodbyes to Bud and Annette. I hadn't thought of it. Wait, was it related?

"God, I don't know. Listen, we need to get a move on.

If he's still coming, he won't be too far behind us," I told her.

"You know what direction we're going?"

"Sort of," I told her, and unclipped a brass compass that had been on my backpack forever.

I pulled it off and shook it as I watched the bubble of air inside slosh around. The needle went back to pointing north. Good. I could already feel the air heating up, and soon it was going to be hot. Yesterday we'd missed most of the heat having driven through most of the day, but the weather app on my phone said it had been in the high nineties yesterday to fall into the sixties at night. It wasn't exactly cold, but it was a big swing from when we went to sleep to when we woke up not too long ago. I clipped the compass back on.

"Tina, we can try going back the way we came. Maybe see if he's cleared out?"

"I don't know what the point of that would be. We still have to find somebody and get help. The van's out of commission."

"You're right. I know you're right. I think Opus could help us find our way back, but maybe that's what he wants?"

"That's not what I'm worried about," Tina said, standing up and putting her pack on, leaving the rifle leaned against mine.

I handed her the gun when she was done and then closed my pack up and put it on. "What are you worried about?"

"For a while, I could hear him back there. He couldn't run as fast as us in the dark, and I think he tripped a few times. I'm worried he's going to keep coming because in

172

the daytime, more people are going to be driving down that road. Unless he left already…"

"Yeah," I said not needing to hear her complete the thought.

With people coming into the park, there would be traffic. We wanted that, but if somebody heard the shots and called the police… It was a double-edged sword. The van, tent, and supplies were back where we'd fled from, but that's also where he'd started with us, and it sounded like he had a dog…

"The dog is tracking us," I told her softly. "That's the only way he could have found us in the dark without using a flashlight. He must have gotten close and realized we were both awake and—"

"Tried to kill us." Tina shivered despite the temperatures.

"What if we make a loop and come back out on the road we parked on. You know, circle around?" I asked her.

"We're going to need water. Do you have a map in your big bag of tricks?"

"No, I left them in the van," I said softly. "But I remember the Colorado River is due east from here. So is the expressway, and there are all kinds of washes that might still have water in it. I can't say for sure that going that direction can be done in a day because I don't know how far we've gone."

Opus yawned, and I got the hint.

"He wants us to move," Tina said.

"Yeah, and anyplace is better than out in the open. We need to find some shade when it starts getting bad, or we're going to go through what little water we have left in a hurry."

Tina nodded and, after a moment's hesitation, I knew I had to make the choice. East to the river and stop a passing motorist? Or circle back around toward the van which was disabled - and possibly the guy who'd shot at us. The van did have water though, and somebody out there camping must have heard that full magazine shot off in the middle of the night. People had been camping within a couple miles of our location. Would they have called the police? I had a general idea of the way we'd come, but the red stone of the mountains was still off our right shoulder, and there was greener ahead of us, though it was now more bushes than trees.

"Ok, we're going to circle around and head back for the van," I told Tina. "I know I've got more water in there and people were camping along the road. Maybe we can run across somebody with a satellite phone, or a hiker."

"Okay," Tina said, and turned to Opus. "Make sure nobody sneaks up on us. Do your super dog growl thing again when they get near."

Opus chuffed, and we set out at the sound of an excited bark somewhere behind us.

"Crap," I muttered, and moved forward faster.

20

RICK

We kept alternating jogging and walking for another half an hour without Opus alerting us. Tina and I had been talking about ways dogs can track. Apparently, the so-called tips and tricks about how to lose pursuit against a dog really don't work. Your body sheds skin cells; dander.

Not only that, but your entire body, clothing and everything gives off a scent. A dog doesn't have to just sniff the ground, their scent of smell is so much better than ours that most of them could track by air if they knew what they were supposed to do.

Opus had been easily keeping pace and now that we were on the greener side I had hopes that we'd find water soon to refill the water bottles, plus the rock and sand were starting to heat up from the sunlight despite the clouds that had darkened the night so much.

"What do we know about the guy who was breaking into places around our house?" I asked Tina who paused and let me come to a stop next to her.

"*Our* house now?" she said, and bumped her hip into me, a small grin breaking the scowl she'd had on her face.

"Yeah, well... somebody takes a potshot at you and your soon-to-be wife, you get used to things quickly."

"Don't get too used to it," she said as we walked. "But not that much. Char and I talked mostly about her date with Detective Stephenson."

"What did she say? I mean about the guy?"

"Fit the description. He's admitted to looking our place over, but hadn't broken in."

"Our place. I like it," I told her, rubbing her back.

"We're going to be in the trees briefly," Tina said quietly. "Hopefully, if my memory is right, the road should be on the other side. We can follow that out—"

Something zipped between us, like a bee on crystal meth with a raging case of diarrhea. The sound of the shot was only a heartbeat behind that.

We both dropped to the ground.

"Opus, get behind some cover," I screamed, as another shot hit a rock near my right shoulder, sending chunks my way.

"Go," Tina yelled, then shouted unintelligibly to the dog.

I felt something brush against me, and sand and rock chunks sprayed my prone form. Something was hot and running down the side of my head. I must be sweating worse than I thought, thinking that the bullets whizzing past us weren't at the firing speed that they'd been fired earlier. Opus had put his head down and was belly crawling to Tina.

These weren't hurried shots, and were barely missing,

which was troubling and it made me feel funny in the pit of my stomach. The adrenaline was once again raging through my system and my ID was screaming fight or flight.

"Let's leapfrog the bushes for cover, he has to be firing at a distance—"

Another shot went whizzing past, hitting about three feet in front of Tina's head. She made her move, and I pushed myself to my feet and took off as two more shots came in. I never heard or saw where they hit, but I felt a tug at my pack as I slid to a stop near Tina, knowing something had happened, but my adrenaline and fear had me high as a kite, ready to run.

"Rick, you've been shot!" Tina said, crawling toward me.

I wiped the sweat off my temple and came back with a red smear. Apparently, I wasn't sweating.

"Tis only a flesh wound," I told her, seeing the fear in her eyes turn slowly to anger. "It was a rock chunk or part of a ricochet. Nothing important was damaged."

Her eyes nearly bugged out of her head. "You've been shot in the head, and that's nothing important?"

"Less arguing, more running like hell," I told her, trying to sound more confident than I actually was.

Tina had the SU-16 out, and in her hands, "I just wish I knew where he was shooting from. I'm a pretty decent shot."

I hadn't heard shots for a few moments so either he lost sight of us or was changing magazines. I was hoping he lost sight of us. Opus came over and brushed me with his shoulder and sniffed the side of my head.

"I know, you think it's funny I'm on all fours like you,

and that I'm at your level. Deal with it and try to stay low, this guy's trying to kill us."

Opus chuffed and then licked my cheek, his tail wagging.

In the distance, a loud shout echoed and wasn't repeated, the words lost over the distance. I could tell by the tone that it wasn't the next-door neighbor girl scouts, or somebody trying to sell us Avon. We leapfrogged from one area of cover to another, always pausing and hesitating and stutter-stepping.

We didn't talk, but it became a habit, and I didn't hear any more shots.

WE ENTERED THE TREE LINE SOONER THAN I HAD EXPECTED. The tree line wasn't what I expected either.

"This sucks," Tina said, staring at the trees we had been working for, hoping for more cover.

"This is not what I expected," I admitted. "We must have been uphill when we saw this."

"It looked like a solid green belt. As long as we head northwest when we get out of here, we should hit the trailhead and hopefully come out near the van."

"That's exactly what I was thinking."

I pulled my pack off and got out my water bottles. I dug around a second longer and pulled out the tin pan from the bottom of the pack and poured out the rest of the first jug of water. Opus was on it as soon as I put it to the ground. I almost chided him for drinking so fast, slopping some water out, but I didn't. He didn't know any better, and if I was parched, he must be dry. I got the second bottle open and topped more of his dish off before taking a long swallow. Tina leaned the pack rifle against my backpack and then stripped out of her pack. We didn't talk, and she killed the rest of her water bottle.

We were both tired and sore. We weren't used to exerting this much energy in this kind of heat. I looked around at the sparse cover. Up close, the tree line was more of some trees with some shrub-looking things, and although it looked green and lush from a distance, it was just a tree or shrub every twenty feet or so. There weren't many leaves, and the cover would be good to break up our profile from the shooter, but there wasn't much ballistic protection.

"Let me look at your head," Tina said and took my water jug out of my hands and set it aside.

She pulled something out of her bag and poured a little water on it. I was about to tell her I had wet wipes in a pouch but it was already done before I could think of it and she wiped slowly at the edge of my temple. I had played off that none of this bugged me, but as she inspected it, her breath hissed in and I felt a stab of anxiety.

"Looks like a cut. A real thin one. Bled quite a bit, but I'm not sure you're even going to need stitches."

"Like I told you, a flesh wound," I told her, sitting still, letting her use the cloth to wipe my face down.

I'd been hot and sweating, and it was cool, wiping the salt from my sweat and dried, crusted whatever off of my face.

"Hey, Opus," I said. "Can you smell him anywhere nearby?"

Opus laid down and put his head between his paws and stared at me, his tail moving softly.

"That's a no," Tina said, "You have a first aid kit?"

"I do, but do you think we should get going again?" I asked her.

"I don't know. I don't know if he's still chasing us. We're—"

"Your kit is toast," Tina said and stopped wiping my face down.

I looked at the open pack. I had dug through it, but I hadn't done it checking everything. The first-aid bag I had was a small thin white plastic affair with a red cross on it. She held it up for me to look at. An oblong hole was punched right through it, and I watched as she opened it.

"We can salvage half of that stuff," I said, my mouth dry again.

"You...this was..."

Tina poked her finger into a hole in the side of my pack.

That wasn't there before, then I remembered when I was hit with the rock chunk when he was shooting at me. Something had pulled at my pack. I leaned forward and spun the pack to face me and then let my head drop when I looked at the far side. The bullet had traveled through my pack, and the compass I'd clipped back on it was shattered. I pulled things out of my pack and found holes in my extra pair of shorts, the first aid kit and a tube tent. If the shot had gone a little bit lower, it might have hit the metal quart of denatured alcohol I kept for my cooker. That would have been bad news... and with the shorts out, I quickly changed out of my sleeping pants.

"You're... he was trying *really* hard to shoot you," Tina

said, and then pushed the pack out of the way and wrapped her arms around me, squeezing me tight.

Opus let out a low *woof,* and we both looked up and around.

"Are you feeling neglected?" I asked him, and he belly crawled over to us. I scratched his head.

"Let's see if we can find the water," I told Tina. "You said there might be a river or a wash just past the green-belt with the trees?"

"Then the road, and maybe help."

"If we can *find* the road," I said, looking at the broken compass barely hanging on to the brass clip on my new perforated backpack.

21

RICK

We moved from cover to cover, but not as fast as we had earlier. The sun was up, and there hadn't been any more sign of whoever was chasing after us, trying to shoot the shit out of me.

Could it have been the bar guy? I might have gone a little overboard with pulling the gun on him when I could have probably stomped on his wrist, but I might have gotten cut, too. I'd just seen a weapon flash at one of my loved ones and reacted. That was problem number two. *Had I been prepared to use it?* That bothered me, because now it wasn't just a loved one who was being hunted by a guy with a weapon, it was *all* of us.

These were the thoughts I wrestled with as the land changed. We were past the green areas to a sharp downward slope.

"Is that water?" Tina asked hopefully.

"Yep," I said, and smiled as Opus let out a happy bark and worked his way down.

The ground turned back into the reddish rocky sand

and clay, and in spots, it was smooth. It wasn't far, but about twenty feet down was a small, fast-moving stream.

"This is one of the washes," I told Tina who let out a whoop and hurried down.

I followed, but not before I looked behind me for the thousandth time. I could see now how much of a rise we'd been walking down. I felt fortunate because the grade had been so gradual that I hadn't noticed it, and we were walking downhill, which was a lot better than uphill.

I made it to the bottom half a minute after Tina and pulled my pack off. Opus was already drinking from the edge of the water.

"This... *This* is what I was really worried about," Tina admitted. "Well, that and a psychotic fan of yours shooting us."

"I still am drawing a blank on that. I've been thinking maybe it was that drunk. Picked up our trail because of Facebook, or maybe he's been holding back, waiting for the right moment."

"He could have gotten us when we were sleeping," Tina pointed out.

"Wait, don't drink that," I warned as Tina was cupping water. "Let's fill up our bottles and use the water purification stuff."

She gave me the stink-eye and splashed the water over her face, then poured it down her arms. I shrugged out of my large pack and did the same, pulling my shirt off.

"Guys are so lucky," she said to me, "Walk around without your shirt whenever you want."

"You could do that. I won't mind," I snarked back, and

ducked as she sent a splash my way, making Opus bark excitedly.

"*Shhh*, sound carries better over water," Tina hushed him.

Opus suddenly found the water interesting and then stepped into a shallow spot that had been made when sand and silt had formed against part of a gnarled branch that had come to rest in the water.

"Yeah, you don't want to hike without a shirt on," I told her, putting my shirt in the water and then pulling it out, wringing most of the water out of it before putting it back on.

She looked at me a second, then pulled hers off, too.

"You really don't have to strip for my benefit, in fact, I think—"

"Evaporation," she said, mimicking my actions. "Works for both guys and girls, and there isn't anybody out here to see."

Opus chuffed, and I shot him a dirty look.

"How about we refill our water and find somewhere in the shade for a little while, rest up, eat, and make a plan."

"You have food?" Tina asked.

"Yeah. I haven't checked if the bags had any holes in them, but I *had* food."

Tina grinned, and I dug into my packs, pulling out two family-sized Mountain House freeze-dried meals on the ground.

"Just add water," I told her, and caught a face full of water as her second attempt to splash me caught me off guard.

I KNEW A FEW WAYS TO SANITIZE WATER TO FILL OUR containers with.

One way was to use bleach. Eight drops per gallon. Let it swish around and then air out for half an hour. It doesn't taste great, but it works.

Another way was iodine, though I didn't have any of that and I couldn't remember how much to use anyway.

What I did have were the purification tablets that were made from iodine. I kept those in a Ziploc baggie inside a Mento's tin. I made sure every container we had was full of water and then put the tablets in, letting them do their thing while I did the last method of water purification.

"When is it going to boil?" Tina asked as she pulled her wet hair into a bun on the back of her head.

"Soon; you know what they say about a watched pot?"

Opus made a disgusted sound and stood in the shade of the tree. After a second, he shook his coat out for the third time since we dragged him into the stream. I turned my head, so I'd miss the worst of the spray and looked down. I'd used my small alcohol stove. It folded down into itself into a small, compact pack. I'd put it together and set it in a more or less level area and fired it up with a cartridge I'd filled with distilled alcohol.

It was perfect for this sort of use. I'd used it a few times already and had come to love it. The tin cup I'd put in there held roughly four measuring cups full of water, and there was already steam rising off it.

Once the bubbles started, I did a mental countdown as Tina looked at it hungrily and tore into the top of a

Mountain House Pouch. It was the Beef Stew packet. Once I'd reached a minute, I took the packet from her and then poured the water in before closing it up and setting it down between us.

Opus whined, making a pitiful sound.

"You hungry, boy?" Tina asked him. His ears pointed almost completely forward, and he barked.

"*Shhh*," Tina said, and dragged her pack close.

She pulled out a gallon-sized bag with brown, round objects filling it. It took me a second to realize it was the fancy *Blue Buffalo* dog food. She opened the bag and then grabbed the tin we'd been using for his water and poured half the bag in. The fuzzy kid drooled the entire time she was doing this, and for a moment I wondered if he was so hungry he envisioned us as pork chops or—

"How long do I have to wait?" Tina interrupted my thoughts.

"Probably ten minutes or so," I told her as I walked down to the stream, filling the still hot tin mug before turning.

I scanned the area we had fled from. I'd spent a lot of time looking in that direction and had come up empty. We'd decided after getting water and eating that we'd see how hot it was out and then decide if we were going to wait and rest, or if we're going to figure out how to get out of there. By my best estimate, it was noon or thereabouts, and it was hard to figure out where we were going without the sun and the moon and...

"Took you long enough," Tina said, as I sat down and put the mug back over the flames.

"Sorry, was looking back there. What do you think,

we've been resting an hour... hour and a half now?" I asked her.

"Yeah," Tina said after a moment. "We've done your water trick twice now."

"The sun is right overhead. If we wait a little bit, I can probably figure out which direction is which."

"You said the Colorado River is to the east of us."

"Yep," I told her, and watched as she opened the pouch, using a spoon to start stirring things up.

"So, if we follow the stream here downriver, there's a good chance it'll take us east where it empties into the Colorado River."

"That's... you're brilliant," I told her and flopped down, spilling some of the water from the mug, and then put it back on the camp stove.

Tina was silent for a time, then remembered the food and pulled her pouch to her side and opened it, letting the steam escape. I wanted to point out how funny it was to eat steaming hot food while it was almost 100 degrees outside, but decided to bite my tongue. I was starving, and I knew we'd need the calories after the morning we'd had and the bruises, soreness, and dings we'd gotten.

Oh yeah, and Tina still thought that getting hit by rock chips counted as being shot in the head.

"So," she said around a mouthful of food, "You want to move out when we're done here, or wait for the sun to go down a little bit?"

"That's what I've been wondering. Now that we know where the water is, we should be ok to do either. Water was the biggest worry of mine," I admitted. "Well, except for getting shot and buried out in the desert."

"You were already shot. Can you imagine the

publicity you're going to get once we get out of this? Famous writer gets shot in the head, leads the family in a trek to survive an insane fan gone wild."

"Please don't," I asked her quietly as my water started to boil.

I let it bubble, but Tina didn't wait long.

"What?" she asked me softly.

"I'm just a guy. I just have a job that's a little different."

"And you're good at it. People read your work, and you're famous."

"I'm not famous," I muttered.

Opus sneezed, and I rolled my eyes at him, Tina catching the look I was giving him.

"Okay, so you're not like *Oprah* famous, but you're like what's his name, the guy who plays the friend of the friend in the TV show *Friends*."

"I don't know who that is," I told her.

"Exactly! To your fans, you're famous. To the rest of us, you're just an adorable husband-to-be - once you meet my daddy, if he approves."

"If?" I asked her, raising an eyebrow and using a spoon to stir the water as it came to a full boil.

"Well, you know, daddy has funny ideas, but he'll totally like you," she said in a hurry.

"Great, something else to worry about," I muttered, and dropped the spoon in the cup so I could tear open my own meal pouch and pull out the oxygen absorber.

I'd got the hot water in when Opus whined. I looked up and around sharply, but then I noticed he was staring at my food pouch and licking his lips. Since Tina had had her pick, I went with the stroganoff. I looked up at Tina who was watching both of us, and I caught Opus belly crawling in my direction.

"You've got your own food," I said, pouring the hot water in the pouch and then closing it.

He begged again, but I stirred it some, sealed the pouch closed and then went about putting out the fire on the small stove. I had to wait for both of them to cool and the water to do its job in the food, so I looked back at Tina.

"You know, for an introvert, the idea of being famous is a little bit—"

"Terrifying?" she finished.

"Yes, but it's weird. Almost every writer I know is an introvert. It's not that we hate people—"

"You just want to do your own thing and not have the massive, confusing mess that everyone else brings to the table, spilling over into your life and—"

I laughed. "You do know me pretty well."

Opus barked an agreement, and I reached over to pet his head. I was rewarded by him licking the spoon I had just used.

"You got to be kidding me," I told him, and he just looked at me, and Tina snorted.

We were lost, in the middle of the desert, not too far from help, being hunted by somebody who wanted to kill us for some reason, and we weren't screaming in blind panic and terror. In fact, we were having a little bit of fun. That said something about our sanity, though I wasn't sure I wanted to know what.

I wiped the spoon clean, poured a little water over it to wash off the Opus germs, and then dug into my food.

Tina and I didn't talk for a long, long time. We just savored the food.

With the hunger and fear combined, it might as well have been a four course gourmet meal, served at the finest restaurant.

"I can't finish mine," Tina said, after a small sip of her water.

"If Opus doesn't want it, I'll take it," I told her, still feeling a little hollowed out, but not wanting to run on a full stomach.

Truth be told, I hadn't eaten much the night before and there was something about running for my life that had made me hungry now that the adrenaline and fear had left me shaky with relief. The worst seemed to be over, for the moment.

"Where's Opus?" Tina asked.

I looked around. He was nowhere in sight. That anxiety, fear and adrenaline suddenly made what I had eaten not feel so solid in my stomach any more.

22

OPUS

Opus was content that his humans were now fed and watered. He'd eaten too, and instinctively knew it was time to move. He'd had a lot of training as a pup before Tina, and hadn't really thought about what he was doing. He had just done it.

When the goofy Two Leg called Rick had started eating, he'd slipped off to the side, pretending to mark his scent like he'd been doing for the past hour. It wouldn't be long now until he really did need to do it, but it wasn't that time yet.

Instead, while they spoke softly, he slunk away into the hot day, slowly at first so as not to draw attention, and was soon reaching a speed that he hadn't done since before the loud bang and pain in his shoulder had prevented him from running full out.

Now he *was* running full out, and not away from the loud bangs that kicked up rocks and sand like it had earlier. Instead, he was running toward it. In training, the men with the large cloth arms would use such a device, sometimes one that fit in one hand, sometimes a larger one that fit in both. They used to be toys and targets to him, until one of them stung him, giving him pain that had lasted and ached until this day.

Opus hated the thing that made the loud bang more than anything in the world, anything except for the people who would hurt the humans he owned. It wasn't just his job, it was his love, his entire reason for getting up with a happy tail wag. Years of taking care of his woman had been repaid with kindness when he was hurt, and he wanted and needed to once again prove to himself and to his humans that he was on the job.

He could smell the four legs. She was with the man who was making the bang sounds, the one who had hurt his man human. He ran toward them, knowing the female four leg was directing the man toward them. She probably had some of the same training he did, but she smelled young. Very young. It was that and the fact she probably hadn't been training very long that he was banking on, if he knew how to bank.

Running, he had covered a lot of distance and hadn't heard his humans calling for him yet. He would have ignored them, but it would be difficult to avoid those he took care of. They were his responsibility, but this was also his responsibility.

Stopping to smell the wind, he got a good idea what direction the two were coming from. It was time. Opus left large scent pools around several shrubs, enough that it stung his own nose. Then he took off in a direction that was between his humans and the one who was pursuing them, leaving spots where his scent would linger. He knew the female four leg would have to smell that; he was on top of his game, and she was near her heat.

He spent an hour marking areas in the wrong direction before he started backtracking and ensuring his bladder was emptied before he ran across the rocks, back toward the scent of his humans. He was going to go a different direction, but was hoping that he'd put down enough of a scent distraction to buy his people enough time to get out of the area. He suspected that if they hadn't already moved on, they would soon.

He picked up the pace, muscles burning.

He felt good, he felt confident. He would lead his people out of this place where there was little water and everything smelled and felt hot and burned, with almost nothing green to break up the landscape.

23

RICK

"I think we lost him," Tina said, after a while.

"We lost Opus too," I told her, surprised that she was so flippant about him taking off or getting lost while probably finding a tree to mark.

"I told you, he'll find us. He's never taken off like this before, but he'll be back soon."

I fumed, not quite angry with her. He'd somehow wormed his way into my heart in a way that I couldn't have imagined, the same way I'd never set out to find a wife who disarmed me with how easily she loved me, quirks and all.

We'd been walking along the stream, or close to it. Sometimes it would cut deep into the rock and earth, and there wouldn't be any way for us to stay near the water without being *in* the water. Still, it was narrowing, and soon it would run out. *I think.*

"I think we lost whoever's chasing us," Tina said, being more specific this time.

"I haven't seen or heard anything," I agreed.

"I'm glad we decided to wait, it doesn't feel as hot now," Tina said, walking slightly ahead of me.

I heard a small bark and spun to see Opus running toward us. Tina let out a surprised squeak that sounded like she held back from yelling his name. I was surprised and amazed that he was suddenly back and had caught up with us. He was running hard and I could see that he was getting dehydrated as he slid to a stop in front of us.

"Opus, where have you been?" Tina gushed as he pushed his nose into her hand.

He made a happy grunting sound, and I was already pulling my pack off to get the large tin I used for his water dish.

"What were you thinking, buddy?" I asked him as I put the tin on the rocky ground and filled it.

He jerked his head out of Tina's hands as soon as he heard the water pouring and lapped it up. I took the opportunity to run my hand through his mane, feeling the heat that was trapped close to his skin. I could see his nose was dry.

"I told you he'd be back," Tina said with a smile, but she had a tear streak down from her left eye.

"I know, he's a good boy," I said, petting him and using my right hand to refill his bowl again.

He drank that down then belched quietly and looked at Tina expectantly.

"You ready to get out of here?" she asked him.

Opus chuffed and walked to her, pushing his head back into her side.

"I think he missed you," I told her.

"He's my buddy," she said, not quite calling him her baby, but if I were asked, I would have no problem calling him a fuzzy kid. "He's hot. If we find a spot that we can get to the riverside safely, let's dunk him."

Opus sneezed and I laughed. He hated his bath but didn't complain too loudly.

"I think we got lucky and the clouds came out more. It looks like it might rain," I said, noticing the clouds as the sun hid for a few moments.

"That's what you said a little while ago. I don't know if it will."

"Hey, do you hear that?" I asked her suddenly.

The noise sounded like a motor. The noise rose in volume and then fell away. Then it happened again.

"We're not that far now," Tina said shooting me a smile.

I looked around and then looked back at the green belt we'd come out of. It was a ways back. I knew this entire time we'd not been any more than a mile or two from a road or a river, but without a compass during our get-away in the dark, we could have been going in circles. Now with the compass busted, I was using the sun to give me an idea and I sort of felt like we were heading south now.

"I can't wait to get off this slope," I said, looking at the reddish hued rock we'd been walking along.

"You're lucky you've been doing more cardio with Opus and me during the last year," Tina said, only slightly less out of breath than I was.

With the water in sight, we hadn't bothered rationing it, mostly just concentrating on getting out. I heard a horn, then the murmur of voices. I looked ahead and saw that the rocky slope we'd been following was turning a corner and there was a shelf we could walk on near the water, built up out of the sediment. I couldn't see anybody, but I knew we were close, right after this corner.

"So, what are you going to say to my dad exactly?" Tina randomly asked.

"I uh... Well, I was going to ask him if I could marry you?" I asked her stupidly.

"No, I mean, *how* are you going to say it?" She asked, and paused to look back at me.

I stammered a second, realizing there had been a fatal flaw in my plan. "So, tell me about your parents," I said, after a long hesitation.

"Well, you've talked to my mom on the phone. She's pretty old-fashioned, but she always was proud that the mini-storage was her idea."

"It was?" I asked.

Tina nodded. "Even though she worships the ground my dad walks on, she has an independent streak a mile wide—"

"I wondered where you got that from," I interrupted, and Opus chuffed, which I took as a chuckle.

"Well, when Daddy went off to war—"

"Wait, your dad is a... was a...?"

"Yeah. The first Gulf War was his last two deployments. He was a career soldier, but mom and I didn't always move around with him. I guess we did when I was first born, but I don't remember it. We came back to Michigan before I could remember too, so you know, it's all I've known. But once he retired, they both worked the mini-storage."

"And when they retired, you took over."

"Well, I grew up working there, and they'd invested well, and Daddy has his pension. So, when I got the business from them, it was kind of all I knew. That, and all the games of paintball and laser tag with the guys growing up."

"I bet your father approved of all the war games," I said with a grin.

She turned around to see if I was teasing her or not, but I wasn't, I was being sincere. To me, it made sense a little bit. She was a very feminine lady, but she had a tomboy streak. She didn't always play it up around me, but at times it shone through. Like her knowledge of firearms, and how she'd comfortably unboxed and cleaned up the new bug-out bag gun I'd picked up. It also made sense when she had a psycho ex who'd made her feel helpless for the first time ever, leading up to her getting Opus.

"He actually thought I should have had my hair braided, wearing dresses all the time. No idea how he and my mom got along," she said, and then snickered.

They were two peas in a pod, that's what she meant. Old school. From a different era, like Old Sarge & Annette.

"How old are they?"

"I was their miracle baby, so they were a little older than most of my friend's parents. They aren't Sarge's age, but probably within ten to fifteen years."

"Oh, ok. Anything I should know? Likes, dislikes... should I—"

"Just be yourself. I think you'll be fine, but if Daddy gets out his guns and starts cleaning them..."

"He wouldn't," I said, shocked.

Opus barked.

For a second, I thought he was excited, agreeing with

Tina that if her dad was cleaning guns, I should probably run, but he barked again, and I saw him wagging his tail.

"Hey there!" a voice called over to us.

Oh crap. I had been caught flat-footed, but Tina was waving back enthusiastically, and Opus's tail was wagging so hard he was almost falling over from excitement. I hurried ahead and caught up with them. The wash we'd been following had curved to the right into what could only be described as a mocha latte frothing, as two bodies of water converged. We'd done it, we'd found the Colorado River and a man was waving and smiling as we approached.

He was a little older than us, wearing khaki shorts, a lightweight white plain T-shirt, and some water shoes.

"Hi!" I said, stepping forward in front of Tina and Opus.

He looked at me, his smile wide as I closed the distance. I could hear Tina engaging the safety as I passed them, and realized I might have been caught unawares, but she hadn't.

"Y'all out doing a spot of hunting?" the man asked.

"We've gotten ourselves in a bit of a jam and don't have our cell phones," I called back.

"Don't tell him we're being hunted by a killer," Tina said coming up fast behind me, her words coming out in a hiss. "He might not want to help."

"Well, come on over, I've got mine in the canoe!"

I looked to my side and saw Tina and Opus had been matching my pace and were right on my heels. It took everything I had not to run toward the man, closing the distance and putting an end to the crazy day we'd had. We were so close now, shouting wasn't needed, and Opus let out a happy bark. I understood his excitement too, it was all I could do not to wiggle as I moved.

"Thank you," Tina said, beating me to the man, and shaking his hand, giving him her 10,000-watt smile.

"We were out doing some plinking and got turned around a bit. We've been out here since this morning."

"Where did y'all come from?" he asked.

"We were at the Arches," I told him, stopping beside Opus who was still showing his enthusiasm with his tongue hanging out the side of his mouth and wagging his tail.

"That's a good bit of a hike. Four or five miles I think. Come on back this way, I tied my canoe off. You need a ride back to your spot?"

"Actually, if we could borrow your phone."

"For sure! I've been up north here for a couple weeks now. Pulled my RV with my wife Greta and we've been seeing the sights, and I've been doing a little bit of fishing. You two on vacation, too?"

"Sort of a pre-honeymoon," I told him.

"Pre-honeymoon?" he said, his eyebrows raised, and then when he got it, an embarrassed grin broke out.

"I'm Tina, that's my fiancé, Rick, and this guy here is Opus. Opus, say hi!"

Opus barked once, excitedly and the man put his hand in front of him without hesitation. Opus sniffed his hand and then jumped on his hind legs and put his paws on the man's chest and licked his face.

"I'm... *Ouaaaffff*," he stammered, as Opus got him.

Opus got down and chuffed.

"I'm Clive," he said, wiping the back of his hand across his mouth to wipe away the dog slime.

"Thank you, Clive," I said simply.

Tina unloaded the rifle, removing the magazine, then racking the slide, catching the shell and putting it in the magazine before breaking it down and taking off her pack.

"Where's the road?" she asked.

"Across the river," Clive said with a grin.

CLIVE HAD STOPPED HIS FISHING FOR A BATHROOM BREAK, and that was how he'd ended up on this side of the river. The campground was more of a wide spot where people pulled off and parked, but there was a place a little further south of that where a real campground was with full hookups.

As we walked down the river bank, we saw people floating down the river on tubes, some laughing, some splashing, and some holding cans that looked suspiciously like Budweiser.

My mouth watered at the thought.

"There she is," Clive said, as a green fiberglass canoe came into view behind a small bush where he'd tied it off with a length of nylon rope.

Other than a bucket of water in the middle with two fish in it, the canoe was empty except for a set of paddles and two life jackets. Clive got in and walked to the back of the canoe slowly. When he got in the back, he dug under his seat and slid out a tackle box that he promptly opened. He dug around and pulled out a Ziploc bag and walked back toward us, opening it as he went.

"Damn," he muttered. "It got too hot and shut down,

or the battery is dead." He held it up, showing me a black screen.

"Oh, that's—"

"I can plug it in, or we can use my wife's if you guys want to take a trip across the river. It's slow this time of year."

"We'd love a ride. Can your canoe hold all of us?" I ask, knowing my pack was starting to feel like it was full of rocks and lead weights.

"Oh sure, I take this fella out duck hunting, and we pack four of us guys in it, and my buddy, Janesh, is a big 'un. Easily tops out pert' near four hundred or so."

"That's fantastic, we'd love your help," Tina said.

He grinned back at her and then remembered I was still there. Opus barked happily, reminding all of us he wasn't the third wheel, and to prove it, he walked back up to Clive and licked his hand and then sat on his haunches and whined expectantly. Clive scratched his head and turned and headed away from us.

"We're so almost out of here," Tina said, shouldering her pack.

"I know, I can't wait to call the authorities and then get this over with. Get the van, spend the next week or so not running through the desert..."

"Meeting my father," Tina said, bumping me with her hip.

"On second thought, running through the desert wasn't all that bad," I admitted.

Opus sneezed, and that made me bust up.

"Are you sure we aren't overloaded?" Tina asked, as Opus stood between us. Our packs were on the floor at our feet.

"Maybe a little bit. If the river was a bit faster and we were trying to go straight across we might have some issues, but trust me, we're fine. You all right paddling there, Rick?"

"Yeah," I told him. "Tina, no worries, you could fit another guy in here as long as the current didn't have white caps. Plus, we're heading downstream. Right, Clive?"

"You got it. I should have you to a phone in about twenty, twenty-five minutes or so. Then you can call whoever you need to."

"Probably the sheriff," Tina mumbled, though she wasn't very quiet.

"You two in some kind of trouble...or hurt?" Clive asked. "Shoot, I didn't even think to ask when you popped out of that incline all sweaty and happy-like."

"Well, we had some car issues, and somebody was shooting near us," I said going for a watered-down version of the truth. "It surprised us, and we got turned around a bit. Once we saw that small stream, we figured we'd follow it, and it'd eventually take us out to the Colorado where we could find help."

"Oh, *phew*. I was worried for a moment, though I might be giving an ax murderer a lift."

"I'm not an ax murderer," I said with a chuckle.

"Wasn't meaning you," Clive shot back.

A surprised look covered Tina's face, and her mouth dropped into an O-shape while she fought back saying something extra snarky. Instead, she reached into the water and smacked it, sending a splash back at Clive.

I snickered, and Opus let out an excited bark as Clive laughed, wiping water off his face. Tina turned around to see how bad she got him at the same moment he slapped the water with his paddle. Both of us got drenched.

"Maybe we are a little full," Clive said, and Opus barked again before sitting down, his whole hind end shaking as his tail wagged.

The ride took a little longer than expected, but the splash fight only lasted a couple moments, the men with the paddles winning of course. Not only did we manage not to go all tippy canoe, the cool water hitting us kept us cool as a light breeze began to blow. It also worked as a tension breaker, and my muscles were sore from the hiking, but I realized a lot of that had been the fact I'd been fleeing with my loved ones from somebody lobbing lead at us from a long ways away.

"Here we are," Clive said, right before the front of the canoe pushed up onto a mixture of rock and sand that formed the bank at the other end.

"Got it," I told him, jumping out and gently pulling the canoe up a little further, making Tina look at me with wide eyes.

"He isn't going to tip you," Clive chuckled, and Opus barked.

I waited and helped everyone out, with Clive coming last. Opus got close and leaped, but as soon as Clive got off, he walked over to him and leaned his head against the man's side.

Clive grinned and gave him a firm pat.

"Give me a hand pulling it up more?" he asked.

"Sure," I told him, and we did, the rocks making scraping noises as the aluminum came out of the river.

"That's good enough." He reached in and grabbed Tina's pack.

I got mine and strapped it on. This nightmare was over. We could call the authorities, get the van, hopefully, avoid any more problems and...

"I'm glad we changed out of our sleeping clothes," Tina said with a smirk.

"Me too," I told her, though my pistol was visible with the shorts and shirt I was wearing.

That hadn't bothered Clive, and as he made a motion for us to follow him, I saw his shirt in the back move and saw the outline of his own pistol. Everybody in Utah, it seemed, was ready for something. Well, unfortunately, that also meant whomever had tried to kill us.

We followed him up the bank. Motorhomes, some as old as War Wagon, were lined up side by side with their canopies open, and on the other side was an assortment of cars and trucks, probably tubers and hikers. He kept a running dialog going with Tina, but I was watching.

Across the highway, the roadway went from flat to a side of a mountain. The red hues in the rock were broken up by veins of some other, sometimes the green of shrubbery. I'd seen snow-capped mountains further north, but this... I realized I was a big dummy. The Colorado River ran through the Grand Canyon. In Arizona. This wasn't in Arizona, but we weren't that far sidetracked, and once we got things sorted out, we'd be heading to Arizona to meet the parents.

"Let me head in and see if Greta is decent first," Clive

said stopping in front of a newer motorhome, its fiber-glass shining.

"Ok, thank you," Tina said, as he walked up behind him. "Or you could just let us borrow her phone and not bother her," she muttered.

The gravel crunched, and a blue Astro van pulled up in front of us, and the driver tapped on the horn.

"Who's that?" Tina asked.

"Hell if I know," I muttered and saw a hand beckon to us.

We both walked up, and Opus made a whining sound, but I wasn't sure if he was complaining we weren't waiting on Clive to come right back out. The passenger side window opened, and I walked over to see what they wanted. I put my hands on the frame and leaned down to see who it was and ask what they want.

I was met with the bore of a large shotgun.

"Get in," Craig said in a snarl that was so quiet it barely left the van, though Tina immediately stiffened by the feel of it when she saw the shotgun.

"Craig?" I said in shock. "What are you doing, buddy?"

"You get in. Tina, put Opus in the back, then load up the packs. If the old man comes out, get rid of him, or your fiancé is going to be the first one to die."

"Craig?" I said again, unable to believe my eyes and ears.

He clicked off the safety.

I believed it now. "Getting in," I said, opening the side door.

"Leave your pack on the ground," he said, moving

from the driver's seat and stepping over the center console.

For a second, I thought he was putting the stubby shotgun right up my guts when he did that, but I saw it was because he was moving. I dropped my pack and wondered if he could shoot through the body of the van.

Could I get away?

If he was the long distance shooter... he *had* to be. Why was he doing this?

"Don't hurt him," Tina said, her voice shaking.

Opus growled. At first, it was the nervous growl we'd all heard before, but within moments it was angry and threatening.

"Opus, come," Tina said, and the volume of the growl increased.

"Close the door and roll up the window, Rick," he told me, and I did, slamming it.

"Clive, a friend, found us," Tina yelled from the back of the van.

I turned to see she'd dragged my pack, and an unhappy Opus, to the back of the van and was walking near the back door.

"Take your pistol out slowly and hand it back between the gap in the seats and the side door. If you turn around during this, I'll end you right here, then hunt down your lovely *wife-to-be*."

His words chilled me.

Where was the guy who'd been joking and hanging out with us a couple of days ago? I reached over slowly, not wanting to die, and handed my gun back between the tight gap. I realized suddenly why he'd had me do it that way. By making me get in the passenger seat, he was limiting my mobility, and handing the gun backward in the gap like that, there was no way to point and aim. The Beretta was roughly snatched out of my hand as Tina opened the back door.

"He's gone," Tina said softly.

I could see the door from the mirror, but I couldn't see her.

"Good," Craig told her. "Load Opus in that cage, pile the backpacks on, and then get in the driver's side."

"Or you're going to kill us right here, right now?" I asked, unable to stop the sarcasm to run out of my mouth.

"Yes," he said and nodded his head with aloof confidence.

"Opus, I know you don't want to, just... do it, buddy, okay? Rick is in trouble."

Opus whined, complaining, but I felt the back end move as he leaped in. I heard metal rattling and then Tina grunt as she loaded the backpacks.

"What's this about?" I asked Craig.

"Shut up," Craig told me, then both back doors closed.

I heard gravel crunching and then saw Tina out of the right mirror as she walked up. Her whole body was trembling, and she had a streak of dampness that ran down one side of her face as she held back the tears. With shaking hands, she opened the van and got in.

"Drive north, turn left," Craig said, his voice full of anger and hate, using the shotgun to point.

"Can I adjust the seat? I can't reach the pedals," Tina said.

"If you don't do it faster than the next five seconds,

I'm going to paint the inside of the van here with his guts."

Tina looked at me, her eyes wide, but she was reaching between the seats and found the catch. She rolled it forward and as soon as it clicked she dropped the shifter on the steering column into drive. She didn't spin much gravel, but we left with a heavier foot than Craig had probably been hoping for. I took a chance and turned halfway to see that Craig had taken the seat behind Tina, the shotgun in his lap, his hand near the trigger as he gripped it.

"Craig, what's going on?" I asked again, and heard Opus growl threateningly from the back.

He didn't answer for a minute, but his face was a rictus of rage and barely contained fury. Then he pointed.

"What?" I asked him.

"Put down the visor, Tina," he said.

She reached up for the sun visor and pulled it down into position. A photo fell into Tina's lap. She grabbed it and held it up in front of the dash with a hand that was suddenly shaking badly.

"What's your brother got to do with this?" I asked as the same time that Tina asked, "How do you know my ex?"

24

RICK

L ance had been Craig's younger brother. He'd hung out with us, and when he'd kissed his first girl, he'd told us all about it. It was strange to think about it, I hadn't been as much of an introvert then as I was now, though, in our early teenage years, none of us were who we are today.

Everybody changes.

I had changed.

Craig had changed.

And Lance definitely had changed.

That was when I realized that none of this was about me. I knew I wasn't the center of the universe, but I hadn't seen this coming, at all.

Because I hadn't wanted to further traumatize Tina, I'd avoided the topic of her ex as much as possible. Somehow, I'd missed the news of Lance's death, but it'd happened in prison.

Actually, I'd missed the arrest and everything else. Maybe it had come out after his arrest that he'd been responsible for the torture and murder of the women Tina had told me about. Then again, I avoided the news, I avoided politics, and I tried to avoid people. It was only the last year or so with Tina that I'd been paying more attention.

"My little brother was shanked over a dozen times in the showers," Craig said, his voice a low growl that could barely be heard over Opus's own. "He died naked, alone on the floor, for something he didn't do."

Tina spoke up defiantly. "He kept breaking into my house and tried to kill me! And when they arrested him, they found all that stuff in his trunk," she said through tears, her voice shaking as bad as my hands were.

"Stuff you or the cops *planted*," Craig spat. "My little brother would *never* hurt anybody. He said you were some goody two shoes who wouldn't put out and was probably a closet lesbian. How the hell do you justify him trying to give you a second chance with him being a kidnapper and murderer?"

"I just wanted him out of my life," Tina sobbed.

"Craig, no matter what happens, you know this isn't going to end well for you. You know that, right?" I said, not sure why I was goading him.

"You know, when Tina contacted me about a protection dog, I couldn't believe it. I almost said something to her then, but I thought what the hell, maybe I could work this to my advantage someday. So, I sold her the damned dog. You want to know what's funny?" he asked rhetorically, the shotgun moving in my direction as I was sitting sideways now.

"What?" I asked, my mouth dry. The tremor in my hands hadn't left yet.

"I got a call a week later. My cancer screening wasn't clean. At all. Needed more tests. Needed more medication. Pancreatic cancer," he said after a moment.

"You're dying," Tina said softly.

"What's that?" Craig yelled back.

"*You're dying?*" she screamed at the windshield.

"Yeah, but I'm not going to die alone, am I? I'm sorry you got caught up in this, Rick, but you're going to be a casualty of war, so to speak. See, *you* more than anybody else here understands about losing family. About losing everyone you love. Don't you?"

"Shut up," I said, my anger bubbling up from the pit of my stomach.

"Oh? You have a spine? That's surprising."

"You're holding the gun, that's the only reason I'm holding back. If it was just you and me—"

His laughter interrupted me, and I turned to give him the finger.

I was jabbed with the barrel of the shotgun hard enough to make me see stars, and my head almost hit the side window, the force of the blow was so great. Something warm cascaded down my face and I saw red splatters hit my shirt and pant legs. A pink haze covered my eye as the blood dripped into it. The anger dissolved and for the third or fourth time that day, I felt fear. We might not walk away from this. It didn't look good.

My hand went up over my right eye. The skin under my eyebrow had been split. I winced, put pressure on it and closed my eye, blinking it rapidly, trying to wipe my face on my shoulder.

"Don't do that," Tina screamed at him.

"I'm okay, it's just a flesh wound," I told her lamely.

"None of this is okay!" Tina screamed, her voice had a panicked quality I wasn't happy to hear.

"Ok, there's a turn off in half a mile," Craig said. "Turn right on it and then a quick left at the exit." He acted like he hadn't just split my head open for the second time in a day, the first from the ricochet or rock chip.

I lift my shirt and felt the shotgun touch my ribcage. I froze a second and then pulled the shirt off, careful around my eye.

"What are you doing?" Craig asked me as I felt the van slow down, hearing the *click click click* of Tina's blinker.

"Going to press this on my eye. I can't see," I lied.

"Hurry up, not that it's going to matter in an hour anyway."

I did, and wadded my shirt, pressing it over my right eye. The blood over it was drying, though I'd pulled the wound back open getting my shirt off and it was bleeding again.

"Good, now Tina, in a thousand yards, there's a two-track. Turn right on it."

I'd been paying attention to the roads, and we'd gotten off on a service road that had followed the highway for a little bit before curving sharply to the right as the mountains seemed to be further away from the highway than before. The left had sent us roughly north, if I had my bearings straight, but this next turn was sending us right back to the mountains and nothing else.

Tina turned the vehicle, and I could see a little better with my left eye. We were heading toward the mountains again, more of the shrub and stunted trees littered the landscape. We weren't driving fast, and the crunching of the tires was almost as loud as the rumble of the van's motor.

The *blue* van.

It had been with us most of the trip. I hadn't picked up on it right away, but now that I thought about it, it had been staring me in the face the entire time. I tried to pay attention to Craig, but he was extolling the virtues of his little brother and spouting a manifesto about family and how an eye for an eye applied in this case because it had been Tina's lies that had got him locked up and ultimately killed.

It was important, but my mind was on the discomfort in my back pocket. My Gerber was still there. It was a little larger than legal, a folding tanto-style knife.

It was one of my favorites, and when we were hiking, it had been more comfortable to be in my back pocket than my front pocket, so I'd moved it. Since the boat ride and now the van ride, it was wearing me raw, reminding me of that, the way I was sitting. But, there was no way for me to pull it out and use it without the shotgun going off.

"Opus, buddy, you okay back there?" I called suddenly.

Opus immediately barked back and then another dog barked. I heard Opus make a growling whine sound and then both of them were howling softly.

"Shut up," Craig screamed, and both dogs went silent.

"Who do you have back there?" I asked.

"This is the real funny part," Craig said, suddenly sounding amused. "Remember when I called you guys?"

"Yeah, you left Tina a message about a dog…"

"You're finally getting it," Craig said after a second. "I knew where you were going because of your Facebook posts, and I used the dog I told Tina was available to track you guys."

"But how did you know to break off and drive around?" Tina asked.

"Fish and Wildlife showed up looking for whoever was doing the shooting," Craig said with a chuckle. "I broke my AR down when I saw them driving around and put it in my pack and walked right out with Ophelia. They never even looked at me."

I wondered why he hadn't stuck closer to my van, which was the way we'd been going to head until we got lost, but then he'd probably realized the direction we were going in, and decided to cut us off on the other side after we were worn out and tired.

Damn, I couldn't write bad guys this good and get away with it. In my books, the bad guys do stupid things, not smart things. And in the end, the bear gets his girl, and the girl gets her happily ever after. None of which was looking very likely for us.

"Right here, pull off. Right here," Craig said testily.

Opus let out a growl as the van seemed to shudder to a stop. This was it? This was the end?

"Tina, hand me the keys," he said, and Tina shut the van off, handing the keys back over her shoulder.

He snatched them from her with his left hand, his right still on the shotgun in a tight grip. Once he pocketed them, he pointed at me with the shotgun.

"Rick, out. Leave your shirt."

I opened the door and got out, tossing the bloody shirt on the floorboards, hoping enough would soak into the floor to leave some sort of DNA evidence. The wind was hot and dry, and although I was shirtless, I could feel the areas of my skin that had started to slowly burn before lightening back up as the full sunlight hit my upper torso.

"Back this way," he said, pointing with his shotgun.

I noted finally that it was a short-barreled shotgun, one of the super shorties the Mossberg platform was known for. I walked with him behind me.

"Open the back doors and get the shovel. Tina, you can come out," he said, as I opened the first door. "But if you run, I'll make sure he dies slowly and painfully before I track you down and do the same."

I opened the second door. Two dog crates were in the space where the back bench-seat normally would be. A blanket had been thrown over the tops and backs of them, and I lifted the edge for a minute. Opus was on the right, and he let out a piteous whine, pleading me to do *something*.

"Hey, buddy," I said, putting my hand on the wire of the crate.

He sniffed it, and the dog in the left crate moved, startling me. In the dark, I only saw a shape, but when Ophelia moved, I realized she was a pitch-black Shepherd, almost as large as Opus, still filling out by the looks of her.

She sniffed my hand, and her tail wagged once.

"Get the shovel," he said.

"Where is it?" I asked, turning just in time to catch the barrel of the shotgun across my face again.

I fell, the blow ringing my bell. I'd felt something in my nose crunch and could taste copper at the back of my throat, like sucking on an old penny.

"You don't have to do that," Tina said. "I can see it."

I spit into the dry sand as blood dripped down off my face. The soil was so parched, it beaded in ruby red drops and then was suddenly sucked into the desert. My head was ringing, and part of me wondered if it was from getting smacked around, getting hit by whatever had hit me much earlier, and getting pistol whipped just now... or could I be dehydrated?

I had to think.

I pushed myself onto my knees and tried to stand when I heard Tina cry out and felt something hit me between the shoulder blades.

The pain made me stiffen out, and I managed a choked cry before I could breathe again.

"You're mad at me! Take it out on me!" Tina screamed at him.

I was trying not to black out when a foot came in low and kicked me in the stomach. All the air I'd gotten back after the shock of being beaten down went out in a *whoosh*.

Good news though, I was now on my back and could see them both. Bad news, he kept stomping and kicking me. Craig had the shotgun on Tina, but I couldn't hear his words because Opus was going insane, barking and snarling.

Ophelia barked as well, but I didn't hear the rage in her voice like I did in Opus's.

Sucker better hope Opus didn't get out of his cage—

I ROLLED OVER AND FELT MYSELF GAGGING. I OPENED MY eyes as soon as I vomited. I was still laying on the desert floor, one side of my face burnt from where I'd been passed out in the sun.

"Rick?" Tina asked.

"I'm okay," I said, coughing and spitting the foul taste out of my mouth.

"Don't you go nowhere. I'm about through," I heard Craig say, though he wasn't close.

"Are you—"

"I'm fine," Tina said, and I looked over.

Something was wrong with my right eye; I really couldn't see out of it, just a sliver that had been smeared with red, and my eyelids weren't wanting to move. Out of my left, I could see that she had her arms behind her back and a clear white zip-tie around her ankles.

"I love you," I told her, and rolled away from the vomit and toward her.

"No, no, lover boy. You're coming this way."

My hands touched her side for a moment before I was yanked by my hair and I could feel a round, circular shape pressed at the back of my skull.

"Hole's getting too deep for me to do it without a ladder. Get in," Craig said and then shoved me.

The hole was remarkable in the fact that he could dig it in the rocky, sandy soil. Hard patches stuck out of the sides, but what was even more remarkable, was when I was thrown face first into it and fell four feet, that it didn't hurt when I landed on my side.

It was almost as if I had that weightless sensation of a roller coaster with an abrupt stop on a mattress made of feathers. What hurt, was when he tossed the shovel in, the wooden handle hit me across the back. I felt my nausea rising again and rolled onto my back, getting the shovel in my hands.

I rose to my feet slowly to see the barrel of the shotgun aimed at my face. My everything hurt at this point, and my head was swimming, but I was scared this was it. He could pull the trigger, leave me in the hole and I'd never know what happened to Tina. Real fear made a cold trickle of sweat run down my back and I'm not afraid to admit to myself that I almost sobbed, this was too soon. This shouldn't be happening.

"Dig," Craig said.

I looked behind him and saw Tina. Her cheeks were tear-streaked, and the dust and dirt had made marks like running mascara down her face.

She gave me a nod.

I put the shovel in the dirt and stepped on it.

25

RICK

I dug for twenty minutes, faking that the nausea worse than it really was, but I did have to stop twice and throw up.

"You know, I really am sorry about all of this," Craig told me.

"You're taking your rage out on me, I know. You've not hurt Tina so far," I told him, knowing he was trying to assuage his guilt.

"That's coming, soon enough."

"Whatever happened to you? You know, your brother obviously turned into a slimeball, and he was killed in prison. Tina didn't plant that stuff in his car," I told him after I saw him looking over in Tina's direction.

"He wouldn't have hurt all those women," Craig said, turning back to me.

The hole was now deep enough, just my eyes and the top of my head peered out. Any time now. It might be deep enough, but any time now.

"He did," I said softly. "Listen, I'm not going to beg for my life, but leave Tina alone. Take it out on me."

"She's the one who had him arrested, it's her fault," Craig insisted.

I put the shovel in the ground and stepped on it, leaning my blind side against the wood. I didn't have to pretend nausea this time, it was there, full force.

"Your brother was a kidnapping, raping and murderous son of a bitch. If there's any blame to be had, it should fall at his feet."

"Shut up!" Craig screamed, and for the second time of the day, I heard the safety click off.

"You don't want to do this," I said softly, pulling the shovel out of the dirt, shaking the clump of clay free.

"Oh, yes I do. When you're dead, I'll put Tina in there, and that'll be it. It'll be done, and I can die in peace."

"No, I mean, you really don't want to do this," I told him a little louder. "You probably want to put down your gun while you're at it."

"What are you talking about?" Craig shouted, spittle flying. "There's nobody around..." his words trailed off as I was smiling over his shoulder, blowing a kiss with my left hand.

He looked to the van, and that's when Tina opened both cages and pointed at him and shouted in a snarl I've never heard her use before, "Támadás."

The world slowed down as two furry bolts burst from the van.

Too slow, he was still turning, and the shotgun started to move up toward the path of Tina and the dogs. I swung my shovel like I was going for a home run. Everything seemed to freeze and then start to move like molasses on a cold Michigan day. You know, they say time seems to stop when your life flashes before your eyes, but it wasn't *my* life.

There was about to be a 12 gauge bore pointed at my loved ones, and I could say, time *slowed*. I had time to reflect.

When I'd come to earlier, I'd pulled the Gerber from my back pocket, and when I'd tried to embrace Tina, I'd dropped it at her side, near where her hands had been bound behind her - unbeknownst to Craig.

I'd seen her acknowledge what I'd done with her look and nod. I'd known then even if I couldn't make it out of this, she could. Instead, she'd cut herself free, and at the perfect moment, she'd unlocked the cages of both dogs.

Both?

Ophelia hit the ground half a heartbeat after Opus, but she wasn't turning on Tina, she was following the bigger and older dog who took a leaping striding step, then another. The flat of my shovel hit Craig's elbow as he was starting to line up the shot. The shotgun pointed up as he fired, the round going over everybody's heads. I heard him screaming, the dogs panting, Tina snarling the Hungarian command for *attack* over and over, and then the snarling was coming from Opus, as he took one more bounding leap before Craig could rack the slide.

Opus hit him first, latching onto the elbow I'd just smacked. Ophelia hit a moment later, putting her shoulder into him as she snarled and bit at whatever she could. What I hadn't seen coming, was the moment Craig lost the grip of the shotgun and the momentum and fury of two hundred pounds of dog pushing him over the edge of the hole.

I too, snarled, as his body glanced off me into the pit. Opus never let go. He ripped and tore, only opening his jaws to work his grip in tighter and higher.

Craig screamed as Ophelia jumped down into the hole on top of him and tore into the inside of his leg. Craig raised a fist and tried to try to punch and kick at the dogs.

I couldn't see well, but I could see well enough to shove Opus away and start punching with my own fists. So much punching... so much blood... so much rage... so much fear.

"I told you I could take you if you put the gun down," I screamed, and hit him again.

His eyes rolled up in the back of his head, and Tina gave the command for the dogs to stop.

I stopped too.

I stood exhausted and panting over his limp body, wondering if I had just killed a man. He was bleeding, so his heart still beat, but for how long? I only saw half of everything, but the nausea was leaving me fast.

***

GETTING THE DOGS OUT OF THE HOLE WASN'T EASY. Neither of them wanted me to pick them up, and I wasn't sure if I had enough left in me to do it, but I did.

Before I climbed out myself, both Opus and Ophelia leaned over the edge, and licked my face in concern, not wanting to leave me in there alone.

Tina had found Craig's cell phone in the middle seat. It took the police a good half an hour to find us. All the while, I kept the shotgun trained on the hole. I'd even remembered to take the shovel out. It was how I'd been able to lift myself up, by putting it across both ends.

"Oh, Jesus, mister. He worked you over good," Mike, the ambulance driver and medic, said.

"Yup. Shot, stabbed, kicked, burned, beat, drowned—"

"You're thinking of Rasputin," Tina said.

"Oh yeah, and drawn and quartered," I finished, as Mike worked on cleaning up my face.

"You were beaten pretty badly though," he said.

"You should see the other guy," I told him, feeling tipsy.

"I did. He's lucky to be alive, you and the dogs really worked him over."

"I didn't kill him?" I asked in shock.

"No, but he's going to need surgery to breathe through his nose again if I had to hazard a guess."

"How bad am I?" I asked.

"Stitches for sure. Probably want to keep you a day or so at the hospital for the concussion, bruised ribs, scrapes..." Mike answered.

I nodded, feeling my brain slosh around, making me dizzy, "Makes sense."

"Just as soon as animal control comes for the dogs—"

"Wait, they're *our* dogs!" Tina shouted, startling the medic.

"Oh, I thought the guy you beat up said—"

"No," Tina interrupted. "Opus is my protection dog, and Ophelia is his PTSD therapy dog," she said, pointing at me.

"PTSD, huh?" Mike said, his tone softening.

"After this, wouldn't you have some sort of issue?" I asked.

"True enough," he said, and put a heavy piece of medical tape over a spot then gave me the ice pack back, which I put over my eye.

"Listen. Even service animals can't ride in the ambulance—"

"You can't let Animal Control take them," Tina interrupted, anger and tears erupting at the same time.

"But as I was going to say...in this case, I can tell my boss what happened and then I'll have to sterilize everything again anyway, which I'm already going to do because that other EMT crew needed some supplies. So, if my boss finds out, tell them you put up a big fight, okay?"

"Got it," I told him.

"Now we're going for a ride. My partner, Gary, and I are going to strap you in and then lift you up. The three of *you*," he said to Tina and the dogs, "will ride in the back with Gary."

"Thank you," Tina said and then hugged him, hard.

Gary coughed in embarrassment and Opus whined while Mike strapped me in. I coughed dramatically, and Tina turned to me, a smile cracking her features.

"Jealous?" she asked.

Damn right.

"A little bit," I said.

Opus chuffed, and Ophelia just looked in at me.

"Going to have to work on your manners," I told her, and she tilted her head to the side.

"It's not that you have *bad* manners, but you're really sort of shy and you don't talk to me as much as old Opus here. You gotta get out more. You have to *express* yourself better."

"It's the concussion," Gary said, trying not to laugh, and then I was lifted into the ambulance.

"You think we should we run fluids?" Mike asked.

"Might as well, they're going to have him on fluids, probably painkillers, and antibiotics," Gary answered.

"I'll get it going, take me thirty seconds."

"Good, I'll call it in before we go and give me a shout when ready.

Tina and the dogs climbed into the back after the IV was started, and Opus sniffed at it and was opening his mouth when Tina pulled him back.

"You can't lick it. It's not a boo-boo."

"Boo-boo?" Gary asked her with a grin.

"Oh... go run your siren," Tina said a moment later, exasperated.

I was laying on my back, looking at the shelves, supplies held in place by plexi-glass doors. Letters covered the different compartments glass, obscuring some things, but when I felt a weight jump up onto the bed, I tried to look down toward my feet.

Ophelia belly-crawled up next to me, squishing me a bit as she laid down on my side, her head resting on my shoulder.

"Good to go," Gary called out.

Ophelia licked my face.

"Dog germs. I've got dog germs on my mouth. She licked my lips—"

Opus sneezed, rather loudly.

"Did he just call bullshit? I swear to God he just called bullshit," Gary said, as he burst out laughing.

Opus chuffed.

The ambulance drove out of the canyon, slowly.

———

THE PROGNOSIS WAS GOOD. I'D GOTTEN THERE SOON enough to get the gash over my eye stitched up, but the temple wound was just cleaned and taped the best they could. Something about it being too long to put the ends together. It didn't bother me much, just having my bell rung that hard did.

"So," Doctor Kaleka said, walking in. "Your vitals are good, you're mostly patched up, and your concussion is pretty mild. I want to keep you for twenty-four hours, but I'd say you're fine after that. Check back in with your family doctor when you get home.

"Thank you, Dr. Kaleka," I told her, "What about the swelling?"

"No damage was done to the eye itself. We flushed it out, and the swelling will go down over time. You've still got a good ice pack?"

I pulled it out from the side of the bed where I'd put it to give my face a chance to thaw out.

"That's good. Where did your wife and dogs go?" she asked, looking around the room.

"She took them for a walk. No matter how well-trained they are, you still have to let them go to the bathroom sometimes."

"Of course," she said with a grin. "For some reason, I thought she went to get them food or something like that."

"Oh, she might be doing that, too," I told her. "I was

taking a nap, and she told me she was going out, but I must have missed her exact explanation."

"That's good. One more thing, the media…"

Oh crap.

"How many?" I asked.

"All of them, I mean, all the major networks. They want to know if you'd give a statement."

"I don't know. Isn't that something my lawyer should do?"

"You *have* a lawyer? I can give them his number so you can get some rest—"

"Naw, I don't have a lawyer," I told her. "Doc, how about not right now. I'm still frazzled and feel beat."

"Well, you were beat, rather thoroughly by the man two doors down from you."

"Yeah." I chuckled. "I hope he gets the help he needs. Guess he had nothing else left to live for."

"Come again?"

"Doc, he said he has pancreatic cancer. That's one of those bad ones that they can't do anything for, right?"

Dr. Kaleka turned and left the room at almost a dead run. Apparently, Craig hadn't disclosed that on his medical forms when they'd checked him in. *If he'd been awake.*

I sat there for a moment, looking at the rolling table the nurse had pushed to the side when she'd come in to examine me again. A white Styrofoam cup full of iced water was just out of reach. I sat up and leaned forward. Inch by inch, my fingers almost seemed to stretch. I'd been in the desert earlier, and my throat was parched.

If I was being honest with myself, it was worse than that. With the screaming, puking, yelling and being parched, my mouth felt and tasted like a baby dragon had used it as a potty chair and it'd had bowel issues. I shuddered at that sudden mental image just as my index finger caught the edge of the rolling lap table.

As I pulled it toward me, a man walked in. He was tall and slender, with a mostly gray spiked crew cut. His black suit looked out of place, and if he were wearing sunglasses, I would have asked if he was with the MIB, but everything about him seemingly screamed FEDERAL AGENT. I almost worried for a moment but saw his hands were gripping a grease-stained deli bag, with a Slurpee cup in his other hand.

"Rick?" he asked, never stopping until he was at the side of the bed.

"Yes sir," I answered and smiled as he pushed the table closer to me.

I grabbed the cup greedily and took a sip.

"So, what was that asshats major malfunction?" he asked, his thumb pointing to one of the walls, in the direction of Craig.

"He was... excuse me, *who* are you?" I asked.

"The guy. Did he just try to kill you both, or what was his reasoning?"

"Listen, mister. I don't know who you are, and I've had a really bad day—"

"Is everything all right?" A nurse popped her head inside the doorway.

"Sure, it's all fine. Right, Rick?" the man asked.

"I thought I told Dr. Kaleka no press," I told the nurse who suddenly looked alarmed.

"I'm sorry, I was under the impression he was family," the nurse said.

"I am." The stranger dug into the deli sack and pulled out two sandwiches, tossing one in my lap and putting the other on the table.

"You are? What's this?" I asked, taking the sandwich off my legs and looked at it.

"The best damned chicken salad on this side of the Mississippi," he said. "Sarge told me when he was laid up that you'd gotten him his fix. I know how horrible the food in places like this is."

Sarge!

I laid back in relief. Tina had put out the bat signal to our loved ones so they wouldn't see it on the news first and think we were both dead. She must have called Sarge and Annette, and he'd made a call to whoever this guy was.

"Sorry, I bumped my head. He's cool," I said.

The nurse shook her head, obviously relieved.

"So, what was this Craig's reasoning?" the man repeated when the door closed.

"Can I eat this?" I asked him, ignoring the question.

"Yeah sure, it really is for you. I didn't spit in it. Much," he snickered then put his hands up. "Joking, it's legit. I don't actually know Sarge, but one of my friends does and *he* called me. I drove straight up."

I dug into it. Before I had always been disgusted with processed chicken salad, but this smelled and tasted good. I took two or three bites before taking another sip of water. So, who was this guy? The food was so good... I decided to trust him for now. If he was somebody Sarge or one of his friends trusted, I should too. Sarge had one time told me about his informal network of friends who had stuck together after they were out of the service.

They would look in on each other, or in odd situations, send somebody to help if they were unable to do so themselves. I'd have to remember to thank him later, when I got out of here.

"When Tina and I got together, we had no idea we both knew him. Craig, that is. I grew up with him, but I've never seen anything like this. I mean, we were friends and hung out, but over time, we just drifted apart."

"I see. You want this?" he asked, tipping the cup he held in his other hand toward me.

"What is it?" I asked him.

"A Monster Slushee made special by the boys' downstairs."

My stomach flipped, but in a good way. I had been refused my drug of choice and my lamentations for coffee had thus far been denied. Monster? A Slushee made of Monster Energy drink? Score!

"Oh yeah, caffeine," I said, and he smiled for the first time and gave me the cup.

I took a couple long pulls but remembered to stop before the icy drink sent bolts of pain through my head.

"Tina knew his little brother. I did too, but I had no idea what he'd done. They dated, and things went south. The little brother, Lance, turned out to be a psycho. Lance went to jail, where he died. That's about all I know. The whole situation is really sort of crazy."

The man stood there a moment then sat on the edge of the bed. I clutched the cup and sandwich and scooted a bit, not only to give him a little more room but to give me a little more room, too.

"Who are you again, anyways?" I asked him. "How do you know Sarge?"

"Sarge was my friend's DI years and years ago. He was his 'war daddy.' My buddy didn't put two and two together until he got Sarge's phone call and started looking up old soldiers who lived near here. I just got in. Plus, I wanted to meet you in person."

"Put two and two together? I'm lost," I said confused.

"Well, you see—"

"Daddy!" Tina shrieked from across the room.

Opus barked, and I lost track of who did what as everything blurred and the stranger stood up abruptly. When Tina got close, she launched herself, and her father (*oh, crap!*) caught her and hugged her hard, spinning her around before putting her down. Opus let out a happy bark at half volume, and Ophelia danced around near my side of the bed.

Ophelia put her head on the edge near me, and I patted my leg. She hopped up gently, turning and then laying at my side, where Tina's father had been.

"Daddy, what are you doing here?" Tina said, tears coming down her cheeks.

"I just got your momma's message as my plane landed. I was golfing the new course when my buddy got ahold of me. I forgot to call your mom until it was too late. I just hopped on the plane and here I am. Your mom is on her way too, but she hasn't gotten my message yet. Her plane hasn't landed."

"Oh, crap," I said, aloud this time, pulling the sheets up a bit.

Ophelia grumbled something, then laid her head across my legs. I pressed the button on the bed to get me sitting up better, and she startled, then went back to relaxing when she realized she wasn't going to be squished.

"How come you weren't—"

"The golf tournament had me out of my usual spot, so the boys and I had driven north to find a new place. Hell, maybe your momma did call, but I didn't have a signal. She's going to skin me alive."

They talked for a while, and Opus came to the foot of the bed then around to the side where Ophelia was. He grumbled, then rubbed his head against Ophelia's side. She turned to him and licked him on the side of the face, and he shook his head. *Dog cooties*. I knew it was a thing.

"So, are you going to introduce me to your dad?" I finally asked.

"Nope," Tina said and smiled sweetly.

I didn't quite fume, because I was suddenly tongue-tied. As far as how I'd pictured meeting Tina's parents, being covered in nothing but a hospital gown after being beaten, pistol whipped and made to dig my own grave... none of it was how I'd envisioned it. *At all.*

"Actually, Sarge has already filled me in all about you, son," Tina's dad said in a serious tone, gone now was the happy-go-lucky man, all around his daughter, he was all business now, "We talked on the phone while I was waiting to board the plane."

Crap, had Sarge told him how long we stayed out in the woods alone together? Or how about—

"He says you're okay for a POG, and that you're either a lucky son of a bitch or a straight up shit magnet that can get himself out of a jam. He can't figure out which."

"Oh, I guess... I mean... Cool. So, can I marry your daughter?" I blurted out.

His eyes bugged for a moment, and a vein I hadn't noticed before pulsed visibly on his forehead. Tall, thin... Probably a runner like Tina, hell, they were all probably fitness nuts. I figured if I ran like hell and screamed like a girl, I might only prolong my life another thirty seconds? A minute maybe, if I wasn't so beaten up and concussed? I really weighed my options for a second there.

"What do you think?" he said, his voice low with a rumble to it that made me think blurting out the question was a bad idea.

Opus chuffed. Ophelia looked up at him, surprised, and then chuffed as well, before putting her head back down in my lap.

"Looks like the vote's unanimous with everybody present," he said and put his hand out. "Welcome to the family."

RICK

"Dude," Al said, walking into the mini storage. "You look like hell."

"I love you too, man," I shot back.

Ophelia sat up, her head above the counter surface we used for our desk in the public office.

"Bro, I'm not like that. Hey, Sonja and Tina... You sure there isn't something in the water, man?"

"Why? You feeling the pressure to go to Mr. Z's and get you a diamond?"

"Dude," he said, his face turning ashen.

I pointed to the chair across from me and he flopped into it, his body seeming to lose enough cohesion to hold him upright with the mention of an engagement ring.

"Sorry, I know you like her. I don't want to push."

"You really think they're looking at rings?" he asked, the surfer persona gone.

"I know they are, but Tina's picking mine out. I went with her once and they got my sizing. She's going to surprise me with it. I mean, I know I'm getting one, I just don't know which one. Don't be surprised if the girls all go goo-goo ga over something they just happened to accidentally see."

"What kind of damage can that cause, am I right?"

"I don't know. First comes love, then comes marriage, then comes momma and a baby carriage—"

"Dude, shut up man," he said, and let out an easy laugh and leaned forward. "So, what about you two? Going to have you some pups?"

"Well, it's too early to breed Ophelia and she has to be in heat first—"

"Naw, I mean, are *you and Tina* wanting to have kids... after the wedding?"

"Back that truck up," I told him, putting my hands up.

"Ha, bro! Now you feel the squirm!"

"You're so twelve," I told him, laughing.

"So, you're doing office duty today?"

"Yeah, I've been sitting here, working on writing stuff and playing around with an outline for something new."

"Oh yeah? No more sexy werewolves and were-bears ravishing the ladies?"

"No," I said with a grin, refusing to rise to the bait. "I was thinking about writing prepper fiction. I don't know much about prepping, as I'm new in the lifestyle, but I can see that there would be a big market for it. Maybe as big as Paranormal Romance? I don't know. I'm going to write a few serials, see how they do, and then tie into some novels into the same kind of world."

"I don't know what you just said, but it sounds cool to me. So, like that one book *One Second After* or *Light's Out*... the one by Crawford?"

"I didn't know you... you could *read*?" I asked him, surprised.

He threw his head back and laughed until his eyes leaked moisture at the edges. Ophelia barked at him, probably in an attempt to tell him to shut up. She didn't have her phonics down like Opus did, not yet, but I could already decipher about a third of her verbal and non-verbals. The rest was just guess work.

"Dude, remember when I got stuck in jail after that protest?"

"The one where I told you to sleep with one hand over your butt?"

The color drained out of his face and for a second he looked like he was about to say something, but the expression broke and he smiled again.

"Yeah man, that time. I couldn't sleep and a dude had that book. Thought they took all stuff off of you when they throw you in the tank, but I mean it was a book, right? So, I read Lights Out. Mutant Zombie Bikers. Man, that was a really eye-opening book."

"I know," I told him softly. "*One Second After* scares the crap out of me."

"Cuz it could totally be true," Al said, back into character again.

"It could. I mean, times are scary. The grid isn't hardened like it should be, and our country's leaders have had a chance to do it, but..."

"That's why you got to get politically active man. Make a difference. Rise up, resist—"

"Hold on there," I said putting a hand up. "That's not likely to happen. I don't like being around a ton of people, and I really hate politics."

"I know, I know, I was kidding you bro. For real though, you and Tina pick out where the wedding is going to be?"

"We did. Her parents are going to fly up here. We're planning on a fall wedding up north, near Sarge and Annette."

"Dude, that's so awesome. So, uh... can I get an invite?" Al asked.

"I was sort of hoping you'd be my best man," I told him. "If you want to stand with me."

"I got your back, bro," he said, a huge grin breaking out on his face. "That means I can do the wild party with the ladies and—"

"Run that one by Sonja first," I told him, cutting his words off.

He made a finger gun and shot it at me. "Dude, I didn't know you knew her name."

"I can't call her Taco Bell girl forever. Besides, I did it to bug you."

"I know man. All friendships have quirks."

Ophelia chuffed in agreement and then walked around the desk and put her head next to his hip. He rubbed her head, scratching behind her ears.

"Opus with Tina?" he asked.

"Yeah. The whole thing with Utah freaked her out. She thought I was in worse shape than I was. She still has nightmares, sometimes."

"Dude, you almost died. It wasn't like some meth heads trying to make off with your food. This dude had you dig your own grave 'n' shit."

"Yeah, for a while there, I wasn't sure I was going to make it. The whole time we thought it was somebody coming after me because of the writing or some sort of... I don't know..."

"Kidnap you to ransom type of stuff?"

"I guess? I mean, it's dumb. I'm just a guy who has a weird job."

"You make shit up for a living, and you make a lot of money doing it," Al said with a grin. "Which by the way, can you loan me some—"

"You know I will. Your raise doesn't kick in until the end of the month, right?"

"Yeah. Assistant Manager. It pays better and it comes with good benefits," he said proudly.

"Yeah, so when you get married and have kids you have everything all covered. Next, you'll need a white picket fence, a dog, three point one kids and a minivan."

"Dude, that might be going a little too far. We're friends, but we're not that good of..." he laughed. "Naw, we're cool, and maybe. I just have to work up the courage. I've been thinking about asking her."

"No kidding?" I asked him.

"Yeah, I know," he said, his voice changing.

He sat up straighter and ran his fingers through his hair, straightening it out. "I guess it's time for me to grow up. I've been just me so long that thinking of becoming half of an entire unit... it changes you in a way, right?"

"Yes, but if you love her, the change is well worth it. In fact, I'd highly recommend it. *If* you love her."

"Damn, dude. Got a beer or something? This convo just got way heavy," he said, persona back in place.

"I do, hold on," I said, and got up.

Ophelia ran to my side and I opened the door separating the house portion from the office and went to the fridge. I grabbed a few Budweisers and walked back out and sat down. Sitting on the desk between us was a stack of money and plastic eyes. I looked up at Al, sharply.

"What's that?" I asked him.

He busted up laughing and reached for a couple of the beers in my hands that were now on the verge of dropping the bottles.

"My little joke to you, bro. Since you scared the crap out of me about sleeping with a hand over my butt, I figured I'd unhinge you a little. If I would have known you were being stalked for real, I never would have done it," he said, twisting the top and putting the cap on the table between us. I followed suit. "As soon as I heard what happened to you in Utah, I wanted to tell you."

"I…" The words wouldn't come.

"I'm sorry, bro. I was joking, but I realized that the timing and optics of that were horrible. I hope you can forgive me for that."

"That was you?" I asked him, draining half a beer in one go and burping as quietly as I could.

"Yeah," he said and looked down at his lap.

"Dude, of all of the things a brother does to another…"

He wasn't looking, so I took the bottom of my beer bottle and smacked the top of his, making the bottle sing out and beer shot straight up, splattering his face.

"Holy shit—"

My laugher cut him off, "I'm sorry, I didn't mean to get you," I said, gasping for air. "I'm not mad, I just hadn't figured that part out yet," I told him, losing my shit and feeling all the remaining tension leave me from the ordeal.

The news came on the TV behind us, and it was replaying what had happened nearly three weeks ago. An intrepid reporter and cameraman had snuck in and tried to interview me the day I checked out and I'd thrown them out of my room, with Opus and Ophelia on either side of me, snarling. The still-shot from the footage showed me in a hospital gown, both dogs with teeth bared and Tina going hulk as she pointed in the lady reporter's face, yelling expletives that would have made Sarge proud.

"With that kind of coverage," Al said pointing at the TV, "I think you can sell *any* kind of books, bro. Never let a good crisis go to waste. Make it your opportunity. It's like politics…"

I gave him the side-eye. "Al."

"Okay, okay. I get it, man. So, when is the official wedding and reception?"

RICK

"Of all the men I've ever had the pleasure, or displeasure to meet," Sarge said, and then paused to catch his breath. "Rick is just about the biggest Johnson-pulling, no account, brass-balled, pencil-dicked..."

I felt like I was about to die. Was Sarge *really* doing this? Could I die from stage fright?

Sarge continued, "...finest young man I've ever met. He might not be a trigger-puller, never served, but he's a fine example of somebody I'd gladly share a foxhole with if he wasn't such a shit magnet— *ouch*!"

Annette smiled sweetly as she put her fork down. Sarge was rubbing the side of a butt cheek. Sonja had a hand over her mouth, whether to hold in giggles or in shock I didn't know. Al was giving Sarge a laughing thumbs up.

"So, in conclusion, I think he's a good guy, and he's going to make her happy, and this is the last time the heart Doc says I can get drunk. *Cheers*!"

"Cheers!" the hall bellowed back, and we all raised our glasses and drank amidst the laughing.

I might have downed all of the champagne in one go, but somebody was quick to refill my glass. I drank it again until Tina pulled my hand back.

"Nervous?" she asked.

"Yes," I told her.

"The hard part is done, silly."

"I know... but there are all these *people*," I said, looking at the crowd.

"Most of them are my family, but there are some people here you might recognize."

I looked at my left hand, at the ring there. Tina's matched, but she had a stone on hers. I immediately thought of writing, and would that extra little bit of weight throw off my typing speed? Tina saw me looking at my hand and placed hers over mine again.

"Time to dance," she said, and pulled me to my feet.

This I could do. I would just stare into her eyes. Hell, I'd been watching YouTube and practicing slow dancing when nobody was around to watch, so I wouldn't trip over both feet. No way. We made our way to the center, where the tables had been pulled back, leaving a dance floor big enough for twenty couples. This first dance though, was ours, and from what my research had told me, then it was the father-daughter, me and her mom... then... the wedding party? So many people here, I didn't know this many people, did I?

"Don't let him pass out," Martin's voice called out from the crowd.

"Don't lock your knees," Karen's voice called.

I found them in the crowd and broke into a smile.

We'd elected to have our wedding in Michigan, and knowing Bud couldn't travel, we'd done our ceremony and honeymoon in the same small town where I parked War Wagon in the summertime.

"Who invited you guys?" I called back, jokingly.

"I did. Part of your police protection," Bern called back.

I turned to find him and real joy kind of hit me. They barely knew me, but they'd showed up. I mean, it had been partly my fault he'd been snagged by the tweakers last year. Still, he'd showed up, and his joke was funny, and he was in uniform.

"I appreciate it!" I called back.

"Now, now, that isn't very proper," Tina said softly as she pressed her body near mine.

I took one hand and placed the other around the small of her back and leaned back a little bit and took in her features. Her gown was perfect, her hair shone and had some sparkle to it. Her makeup was almost nonexistent, just a little bit of highlighting around her eyes, and her shoes...white with a small heel that made Tina seem almost two inches taller.

My breath caught in my throat.

"I love you. To hell with being proper," I told her, and kissed her as the crowd cheered.

After I pulled back, she looked at me funny and tilted her head to the side a little bit.

"You know, you're right."

"I am?" I asked.

"Yes. To hell with being proper," she said, as she let go of my hand and pushed herself back.

The music, where was the music? Weren't we

supposed to be dancing? Everyone was looking, some were smiling, some were whispering. I looked at the head table and saw Sarge staring right back at me, his thumb up in the air. Annette was blowing a kiss, and then a sharp whistle went through the air, so shrill I stepped back a second before realizing it was coming from Tina.

"What are you doing?" I asked her.

"Answering the question first," she said as two furry shapes erupted from under the head table and headed to the dance floor.

"What question?" I asked as Opus and Ophelia came running at us.

"Just like we practiced," Tina told them, over the growing murmur of voices.

"Practiced what?"

"You're going to love this," Tina said with a grin.

"I am?" I asked, as both dogs pressed themselves close to both of us. Opus on Tina's side, Ophelia on mine.

The amplified PA system kicked in, the bass almost drowning out the lyrics.

"Who let the dogs out?"

I laughed, and I looked up at the head table. Tina's mother and father were laughing and standing, and began to dance. What the hell, let's have fun. It was the first night we'd have together as a married couple, for the rest of our lives.

Even then, that might not be long enough.

TINA & OPUS

The furry traitor was now Tina's. Rick had been working with Ophelia every day at the training center, which was really an old farm with five acres fenced in and a dozen K-9 units from the county all coming together, dogs and handlers learning from the best of the best.

Opus was laying down next to Tina, who'd been laying on the couch and listening for the ding of the office's front door. She'd had *Pepto* three times already and wasn't feeling the greatest. For a Saturday, the mini storage had been especially quiet.

"So, are you and Ophelia getting along?"

Opus let out a chuff and then sighed, laying down in Tina's lap, his head resting against her upset stomach. She thought about asking him to move for a second, but the nausea seemed to pass quickly and she sighed in relief.

Opus let out a surprised whine and sat back up, looking pointedly at Tina's stomach.

"I know, I know. I just found out myself," Tina told him, rubbing his head and scratching his ears.

He hadn't missed the worry in her tone.

Opus let out another chuff, then laid his head back on her lap, rubbing his left ear against her belly button this time. It didn't make the nausea come back, but she knew what he was doing suddenly. Tina was built elfin like. She wasn't tall and graceful like her mother, she was more of the shorter, athletic build. Still, she'd barely noticed the small bump that was forming.

They had all slowed down after their ordeal in the desert and Opus once again rubbed his head against her stomach, his ear next to her belly button. It might have been in her mind, but she thought she felt a wiggle again. *Too early to feel it*, she thought, and held up the pregnancy test.

'+ +,' was what it showed.

"Looks like you're going to have another human to help take care of," Tina said, rubbing his head again.

Opus barked softly and rolled on his back, so he could look up at the human he owned. He yawned, then smiled at her, his tongue hanging out of the side of his mouth.

"Do you think I should wait to tell Rick?"

Opus rolled over and got down on the carpet on all fours, looking up at Tina.

"I'm serious. I'm worried. The doctors said I might not ever be able to have babies and I'm worried if I tell him and I lose it..."

Opus sneezed. Tina's tears fell softly.

"You're right. It is bullshit. Let's call him and ask him to bring a pizza home. Then we can tell him."

Opus chuffed.

--THE END--

To be notified of new releases, please sign up for my mailing list at: **http://eepurl.com/cZ_okf**

AUTHOR'S NOTE

I never imagined writing a second Opus storyline when I first penned One Man's Opus. It was my way of healing. When you learn and grow with a fuzzy companion, losing them feels like losing part of yourself. I had to write One Man's Opus as something to remember Beast by and I never thought it would take off and sell the way it did.

Saying all of that, with prodding from family, friends and fans, I decided to Pen another Opus book. This one picks up after the near deadly events of the winter before. I'm not sure if there is another Opus story after this one, but I'm going to let the fans decide. Shoot me an email and tell me what you think.

These two stories varied from my usual prepper post apocalyptic fiction and Opus Odyssey ventured closer into thriller territory than the first one. There was only one thing I thought I could do to make this story believable and fair. Drop the family into a bad situation and then remove all their advantages and leave them the basics. Yes, they weren't lost in the desert long, but for that area more than that becomes a survival story for different reasons than a mad gunman.

As always, thank you for reading the story! Feel free to contact me via Facebook or email at boyd3@live.com and tell me if you want more of Opus & Ophelia!

ABOUT THE AUTHOR

Boyd Craven III was born and raised in Michigan, an avid outdoorsman who's always loved to read and write from a young age. When he isn't working outside on the farm, or chasing a household of kids, he's sitting in his Lazy Boy, typing away.

You can find the rest of Boyd's books on Amazon & Select Book Stores.

boydcraven.com
boyd3@live.com

77687771R00154

Made in the USA
Lexington, KY
31 December 2017